Hearts of Oak

ALSO BY EDDIE ROBSON

Tomorrow Never Knows

NONFICTION
Coen Brothers
Who's Next (with Mark Clapham and Jim Smith)
Film Noir
Dracula (with Nicola L. Robinson)
The Art of Sean Phillips (with Sean Phillips)

HEARTS OF OAK

EDDIE ROBSON

A TOM DOHERTY ASSOCIATES BOOK
NEW YORK

This is a work of fiction. All of the characters, organizations, and events portrayed in this novella are either products of the author's imagination or are used fictitiously.

HEARTS OF OAK

Copyright © 2020 by Edward David Robson

Cover art by Armando Veve
Cover design by Christine Foltzer

Edited by Lee Harris

A Tor.com Book
Published by Tom Doherty Associates
120 Broadway
New York, NY 10271

www.tor.com

Tor® is a registered trademark of
Macmillan Publishing Group, LLC.

ISBN 978-1-250-26052-9 (ebook)
ISBN 978-1-250-26053-6 (trade paperback)

First Edition: March 2020

For Catherine, Gabriel, and Jago

Hearts of Oak

1

THE KING GLANCED ACROSS his chambers and saw his morning letter had arrived. He picked it up from the floor and was surprised by its weight. He turned it over in his hands. "It's a thick one today," the king said to his cat.

"I know," agreed his cat, who was large and ginger and called Clarence. Clarence always delivered the morning letter to the king's chambers, carrying it in his mouth, and so he was bound to notice when it was thicker than usual.

"What's happened to make it this thick?" asked the king, squeezing the letter between his thumb and forefinger.

"Open it and we might find out," said Clarence impatiently.

The king opened the envelope and pulled out the wad of paper that had been folded into thirds. He skimmed the summary on the uppermost page. "Oh right," he said. "All the funerals for the victims of the building site collapse are being held today." This meant the letter would be full of tributes from their friends and colleagues. And one of the victims, a man called Weston, had been a teacher for a long time. People always remembered their old teachers and they often sent tributes. The king counted the dead listed on the summary. "Wow. *Nine* funerals."

"A terrible disaster, Your Highness," said Clarence, shaking his head.

The king sat in his chair by the window, turned to the first page, and started reading.

Clarence sat on the small table by the king's chair. After the king finished reading each page he placed it facing upward on the table so Clarence could read it. But Clarence was visibly disinterested and somewhere around the seventh page he became impatient. "Can't we skip ahead?"

"No."

"I need to read the construction report."

This was sometimes a bone of contention between them. The king was always keen to read about the lives of his citizens but had no interest in the dry details of construction reports—as long as building was progressing he didn't feel the need to know about it. Clarence was the other way around. But the king firmly believed he was right about this and Clarence was wrong—if the construction report was more interesting than the tributes they wouldn't put it at the back.

"No," said the king. "I want to read these first. You've got to have respect for the dead."

"I do have respect for the dead but the sooner I read the report, the sooner I can get on with—"

"Alright," said the king, peeling off pages from the back of the letter until he reached the first page of the report. He slapped these pages down on the table in front of Clarence. "Happy now?"

Clarence purred.

The young woman waiting in Iona's office looked deeply unusual although Iona couldn't pin down exactly what it was about her. She was smallish and sharp-featured, and she was mostly dressed in shades of gray. Her blond hair fell in ringlets from under a red hat. Her clothes were odd—they didn't look like they were made of hemp, which led Iona to wonder what exactly they were made of. She was young enough to make Iona feel very old.

The young woman stood up and took off her hat as Iona entered and Iona told her to sit back down again. Iona walked around behind her desk and lowered herself unsteadily into her own chair. Then she leaned back and asked the young woman her name.

"Alyssa," she replied.

Iona welcomed her and asked why she had come.

Alyssa leaned an elbow on the chair's armrest and leaned her head on her fist. The young woman wore a bracelet with a series of small unfamiliar objects attached to it, which jangled distractingly. "I'd like some tuition."

"My classes are open to everyone."

Alyssa smiled awkwardly. "I was hoping you could give me some one-to-one sessions? I work in planning, you see, and the classes don't give us much grounding in the practical side—they only really talk about zoning space. I don't have time for the full course but I'd like a sort of idiot's guide."

"I've never done anything like that before."

Alyssa raised her eyebrows hopefully. "Does that mean you couldn't do anything like it now?"

Iona thought for a moment. She had learned to accept clashes with the planning department as par for the course: they didn't fully understand how her job worked and didn't try to. Iona had learned to anticipate their foibles and work around them. It seemed churlish to turn away someone who *wanted* to know more. "I suppose I could do it. But there are lots of other people you could ask."

"But you're the best. Everyone learned everything they know from you."

Iona laughed. "Who told you that?"

Alyssa shrugged. "Everyone."

It was true that Iona was the leading architect in the city and had been for a very long time. But times had changed, the city was bigger, its needs were bigger. They still kept her on at the school and she still designed as many buildings as she ever did, but the work had to be shared between more people these days and there were now many others just as skilled as she was. She sometimes vaguely floated the idea of retiring but it was always laughed off. She'd be here until she dropped. Which was fine by her, she'd be ever so bored at home.

Her mind had wandered and she remembered Alyssa was still waiting for an answer. She supposed there was no reason not to do something just because it wasn't how things were usually done.

They made plans to meet here again tomorrow and then Alyssa left.

Alone in her office, Iona drifted off into wondering how she would structure their sessions and it took her a few minutes to notice Alyssa had left her hat behind on the desk. The young woman had probably left the building by now, so Iona decided to just hold onto it and give it back tomorrow. She picked it up.

The texture of the hat triggered something in her. As she felt it she heard the word *felt* in her mind, but she knew it didn't mean *felt* in the sense of *feel*, it was . . . what the hat was made of. Iona didn't know how she knew that. It was a dream-word. Iona saw lots of things in her dreams that didn't exist in the world and she knew the words for them, but she never spoke them aloud because nobody else would know what she was talking about.

She had never before wanted to apply a dream-word to something in the real world, but here it was. The hat was made of felt. It seemed a stupid word and yet she knew it was right.

But there was more. A scatter of tiny, fragmentary thoughts was thrown up by the word, as if something had been tossed into the attic of her mind and disturbed the dust. Flashes of people, places, things that didn't exist but that somehow meant a lot to her anyway, and came at her too quickly to hold onto—

The door of her office opened again and Alyssa entered. She stopped short and looked at Iona curiously.

Iona realized she was sitting behind her desk, holding Alyssa's hat and weeping.

"Sorry," said Alyssa, pointing. "I forgot my—"

"Yes," said Iona, blinking and handing over the hat. "Sorry, I lost a colleague recently. It's his funeral this afternoon." This was true, though it was not the reason for her tears.

"Oh, I see. I'm very sorry." Alyssa seemed to accept this as an explanation and left.

———————

Iona had plenty of time before the funeral so she decided to walk rather than take a rickshaw. As she left the school and walked down the main thoroughfare, King's Tower loomed up ahead of her. It currently had scaffolding all up one side. When Iona had designed it—so long ago now she could hardly remember—it had been a sleek needle shooting from the center of the city and up above the skyline. These days it was swollen by extensions and additions, mostly designed by Iona herself and all to the detriment of the building, in her opinion, though she'd done her best with them.

The planning department, which had long stood in the shadow of the tower, had been scheduled for demolition just as soon as work on the new, larger planning department was completed. In place of the old planning department a new buttress would be built to support the tower on its heavier side. Six more floors had recently been added at the top of the tower, bringing the total to thirty-one, and the king's apartment had been moved so it was once again on the top floor. But before they could build any further extensions they needed to reinforce that side—Iona had been clear on this even though the planning department would have happily signed off a ten-story extension if she'd let them.

Iona was all in favor of tearing the thing down and starting again but she knew planning would never agree to that. King's Tower was sacrosanct.

Iona took a detour past the building site for the new planning department because she wanted to see how it was going. At twelve stories high it was larger than it needed to be, but then that was true of everything these days. Her own house was a prime example. From time to time they would tell her she deserved a bigger one for all her good work; she would tell them she didn't need a bigger one, and was happy with what she had; they would assume she was just being polite, and insist she accept; and she would accept. She rarely went into the upper stories of her current house and when she did it struck her how they still smelled new.

A member of the construction team recognized Iona from a long way off and as she arrived at the edge of the site several of them came over to meet her. She recognized many former students. They surrounded her, their voices tumbling and clattering against each other as they eagerly greeted their old teacher. They asked how she was (she said fine), what the school was like these days (she said it was much the same), if she was going to retire soon (she said they wouldn't let her). In return she complimented them on their excellent workmanship, to which they modestly replied they were just doing things the way she'd taught them. They offered to show her around the site but she told them she couldn't stop, she was on her way to the funeral.

The atmosphere turned somber.

"We wanted to go, we couldn't get the time off," said one of her former students, whose name was Bridge. They asked Iona to pass on their condolences and drifted back inside.

———————

The funeral took place at the city's largest and newest Point of Return. It had been built as a single unit but designed as two units fused together, so it looked like the two sections had been built at different times but it was impossible to tell which came first. This effect was deliberate. As she arrived Iona remembered with a jolt that she and Weston had collaborated on the design.

The memorial parlor at the front was an attractive, old-fashioned building with a high ceiling, a sharply sloping roof, and a steeple at the front with a sundial on it. The restricted area beyond was larger, a featureless semi-cylinder with narrow windows at regular intervals. It was the third Point that had been built since the city's foundation, meeting the demands of a greater population, and no doubt one day the call would come for a fourth, larger still. Iona pondered how she would improve on this one when that day came. You could always improve. There were always needs you couldn't anticipate, you could only watch and see how a building functioned on a day-to-day basis.

Entering the memorial parlor, Iona saw the turnout was good. All Weston's colleagues had come, and as the school was closed for the afternoon, many of the students had come too. The people Iona didn't recognize were, presumably, Weston's friends and neighbors. Rather than walking down the central aisle, Iona went down one side and made her way to the front, where a space had been reserved for her.

The last few mourners filed in, the doors closed, the room went quiet, and the undertaker took up her position at the front. Weston's plain coffin stood open on a table behind her.

"Weston," said the undertaker. "Architect. Teacher." She then gestured to Iona, which was her cue to rise and take the undertaker's place.

Iona looked out across the rows of faces, all angled expectantly toward her. She turned to the coffin and peered in at the body of her deceased colleague. Weston's inanimate form looked as if he might just be resting. The surest sign that he was actually dead was the perfect symmetry with which his body had been laid out. The precision was traditional and unmistakable. Iona reached across and placed her hand on Weston's. It was cold and smooth to the touch.

Iona turned back to the crowd and spoke. "In all my years of teaching, I have had the pleasure of working alongside many brilliant and inspiring people. But few were as creative in their thinking, or as clear in their communication as Weston. He was utterly dedicated to his students. I remember once finding him asleep in the corner of the staff room. The planning department had returned one of his designs with what they thought was a minor change, but actually meant completely restructuring the ground floor—and the plans needed to be revised and submitted to the king in two days. Instead of getting someone else to cover his seminar on load-bearing experiments, Weston skipped two downtimes so he could do both because he didn't want to let the students down. I couldn't rouse him, I had to pull him home myself in a rickshaw."

Some laughter at that image.

"The school is poorer for his loss. So is the city. His contribution, in terms of design and knowledge, was immense. He will not be easily replaced, but he will be easily remembered."

She mentioned nothing about how he'd died. People didn't want to dwell on that.

As Iona returned to her seat, returning appreciative glances with a nod, she wondered whether she had said those words before to someone else's mourners. She had spoken at a huge number of funerals—she was always asked to, if she'd known the deceased—and what she'd just said had a familiar ring to it. Even the anecdote, which the more she thought about it may well have been about a different colleague. She worried that someone in the audience might remember her saying it and find this disrespectful.

But whether she had said those things before or not, she still meant them. And surely nobody was comparing this eulogy with her previous ones and checking for repetition. Those words she'd just spoken would go in no book, they had lived in the air for a moment and now they died just like the man they'd commemorated. The content of them was less important than the feeling they left behind.

A couple more people took to the stage to say a few words, then the undertaker returned, closed the coffin, and with the help of an assistant turned it 90 degrees, so Weston's feet now pointed toward the furnace door at the back of the hall. Then the xylophonist at the side of the stage started to play a ceremonial tune that echoed through the hall as the furnace door slid open, revealing the flames beyond.

(The sight of the furnace never failed to raise a flinch from some of those watching.)

The undertaker and her assistant pushed the coffin onto the conveyor that led to the furnace, then they both stood back and let the slow turn of its rollers draw the coffin along. This was always a moment of contemplation, this final journey to the flames. For some the reality of the loss of their friend would just be hitting home, while others would be anticipating a moment of catharsis, the circle of a life completed. The amount of energy gained by burning the body was minimal, of course—a fraction of what the city required to run for even an hour—but the symbolic value of the gesture was powerful.

However, someone seated at the back of the parlor had something else on his mind. Iona didn't hear him at first—rather, she heard other people turning to look at him and she turned too. The man was standing up and making his way along the pew toward the aisle. He wasn't anyone Iona recognized, he certainly wasn't from the school. When he reached the aisle he started to walk toward the front, then he started to run. Disquiet spread through the parlor but nobody tried to stop him or even spoke up. Nobody had the slightest idea what he was doing so nobody knew what to do about it.

The man reached the front, leaped up onto the stage, and headed straight for the conveyor. The xylophonist dropped his beaters in surprise. The undertaker and her assistant moved to intercept the interloper but they were unprepared and he was stronger than them. He nudged them aside easily and climbed onto the conveyor. The coffin had still not quite entered the furnace. The man dashed along the rollers, leaped onto the coffin—

And the man and the coffin disappeared into the furnace together. The door closed behind them.

The mourners stared at the stage. There was silence. The undertaker and her assistant stared at each other.

Haltingly the xylophonist started to play again.

––––––––––––

The crowds leaving the Point of Return filled the streets, mingling with other citizens, and Iona could hear whispers about what had happened in there. Nobody could explain it. Had the man been suicidal? If so, why choose that time and place and that manner? Did he have some connection with Weston and was unable to accept life without him? Or had he been trying to open the coffin in those final moments, release the body? Some colleagues asked Iona what she'd seen, but she told them from where she'd been sitting she couldn't tell what he'd been trying to do. It had all happened too quickly.

The crowds drifted away from each other and Iona

walked back toward her house, which was a very short distance from the school. As she turned into her street she glanced into the window of one of her neighbors. She could see two people sitting on either side of a table, their attention focused on each other, engrossed in conversation. This was a very common sight across the city, it was how most people spent their spare time, and Iona knew she wasn't meant to look—it was a private thing. She wondered, not for the first time, why nobody had ever invited her to do it with them. She never asked anyone—it didn't seem right to. Maybe she should have asked Weston. If there was anyone she could have asked it was him.

Iona returned home and sat on the bench in her living room. She picked up a book and tried to read, but couldn't focus so she put the book down. The image of that man leaping onto the coffin, the feeling of Alyssa's hat under her fingers—these things kept forcing their way to the front of her consciousness. She tried reading the newspaper for a bit instead but couldn't focus on that either so she reorganized her furniture. Eventually, after hours of turning over the events of a very strange day in her mind, she decided to go to sleep.

As Iona closed the shutters and settled down in bed her unease coalesced into a single thought: when Weston had started working at the school, she remembered realizing there had been a complete turnover in the school's staff—except for her. Now, with Weston gone, there had been a complete staff turnover again. Except for her.

The king looked out across the city. He didn't have a good view out of this window at the moment because this side of the tower was covered in scaffolding. His view was often spoiled by scaffolding. But he could see the Point of Return. At night the light from its furnace could be seen blazing through the windows.

"I feel like I should have gone to the funeral for that Weston guy," he said.

"Why?" said Clarence, trotting over to him and jumping up onto the dressing table. "You only ever met him twice."

The king turned to Clarence, surprised. "I met him?"

"At opening ceremonies. And only very briefly."

"Huh." The king turned back to the window. "He meant a lot to people though, didn't he? There was a lot of warmth in those tributes. Maybe I should have gone down there and told them . . . I dunno, that I liked reading them."

"It might have looked like favoritism, with the funerals of the other victims also happening today."

"I could've gone to all of them. I had time."

"Nobody expects that."

"Hmm." The king felt like it was a long time since he'd had proper contact with the public. He wouldn't say he felt lonely exactly, but . . .

No, maybe that *was* it. Maybe he felt lonely.

"Perhaps I'll write something about him in my column this week," said the king.

"That's a better idea."

"If I'd known more about him I'd have given everybody the day off." The king felt agitated, felt he hadn't done enough. "I didn't realize how big a deal it was for so many people."

"Why would you?"

"It's my job to know this city, isn't it?"

"Look, if you'd given everyone the day off we'd have lost time on building the new planning department."

"Yeah, good point," said the king, nodding and closing the shutters. "If we don't get that built, the city will never get finished, will it?"

2

WESTON'S REPLACEMENT WAS SO eager to get started he was waiting for Iona the next morning in the school's front lobby.

"Hello!" said Carter, bounding forward to shake Iona's hand the moment she entered. "Lovely words at the funeral yesterday—really lovely."

"You were at the funeral?"

"Yes."

There was an awkward moment as each wondered if the other was going to bring up the disturbing incident at the end of the funeral. Iona wanted to talk about it; she desperately wanted to know why it had happened, what it meant. But to take such an interest in something strange would only mark herself out as strange. She knew it was better left alone.

"Anyone who knew Weston would have said the same," said Iona eventually.

"I wish I'd known him—as more than just a teacher, I mean."

"If you knew him as a teacher, then you knew him."

Carter looked around the lobby. "I mean, it's a terrible way to get the job, but . . ." He'd been in line for a teaching post for some considerable time. He had worked fourteen years in construction and his body bore the scars.

"He'd be glad to know his replacement was enthusiastic, don't worry." Iona offered to show him to his new office—which was Weston's old office—where she would give him a rundown of his duties and workload and make sure he had everything he needed. As they walked she became increasingly aware of loud noises—not the usual chatter of students but hammering and sanding. Was there a practical going on? No, there couldn't be—the day's classes hadn't started yet.

As they turned the corner Iona realized the noises came from their destination. The door to Weston's old office had been removed and members of a crew were coming and going. All Weston's books had been removed and stacked up against the wall in the corridor. Iona and Carter tried to step though the doorway but were pushed aside by a bulky man who barely bothered to say "excuse me."

Iona looked inside and saw that half the office floor was missing. The other half was in the process of being torn up. All the furniture was gone, including the filing cabinet, and the shelves and shutters had also been removed. The paneling on the walls was being sanded smooth.

The foreman saw the two teachers and strode over to them. "You can't come in here."

"Yes, we realize—" Iona began.

"This office needs a refit before it can be used—"

"By him," said Iona, pointing at Carter. "It's going to be his office. He's supposed to be here, you know."

The foreman peered suspiciously at Carter. "Thought you weren't starting until tomorrow?"

"Oh sorry," Carter said. "Am I causing trouble?"

"You've nothing to apologize for," said Iona and then addressed the foreman. "Is this really necessary?"

"The school told us to get it done while it was empty," the foreman replied, "and quite right too—it was so dilapidated."

"But now he doesn't have an office."

"The sooner you leave us to get on with it, the sooner he *will* have an office."

Iona sighed and turned to Carter. "I'll show you the staff room," she said and they went back down the corridor the way they'd come. She disliked seeing the last evidence of Weston's presence being removed. The patches of floor he'd worn down by pacing around, the marks on the wall where he'd leaned back in his chair. The traces people left on this city all got removed sooner or later, but for it to happen immediately was a shock.

After her morning classes Iona had a three-hour gap in her schedule, so she took the proofs of the new edition of the textbook over to the park. She'd already gone through more than half of it—it was a fairly light job these days because each edition changed very little from the previous one. Once upon a time the changes from one edition to the next had been very substantial. New building techniques would emerge, existing ones would be refined and improved. But very little significant progress had been made lately. Perhaps there wasn't much left they didn't know.

While writing this edition of the textbook Iona had wondered how it compared to the first edition she'd written all those years ago. There had been so many editions they all blurred into one. She'd gone down to the library and asked for it only to be told the early editions of the textbook had all long since been withdrawn and recycled. Iona wondered why that was necessary. The library seemed to have plenty of space and the textbook was perennially the city's most-read book. But then again, who'd want to read the old ones now? It was vain of her to expect they'd keep them all.

She finished going over the proofs sooner than expected. She put them in the post and decided to take a walk out to the forest.

_____

This part of the forest was midway through its cycle, so it was deserted. At the start of their cycle the trees were given close attention to ensure they grew well; near the end they were carefully checked for disease and then prepared for felling. In the middle they were left to get on with it.

It was good to get away from the sounds and smells of the city for a while—the hammering, the sawing, the burning. These were so pervasive one could easily forget what real quiet was like. The air here was fresh and the only noises were those of the forest responding to Iona's presence: the grass rustling, twigs cracking underfoot.

Iona kept walking until she reached the very edge, the place where the grass petered out into the whiteness of the floor beyond. A meter or so beyond the last tufts of grass the floor banked sharply upward and merged straight into the wall. As ever the wall glowed gently and was warm to the touch. It was smooth and seamless—in all but one place.

Iona walked parallel to the wall: it took her a few minutes to reach the window. As usual a couple of citizens stood by the window, contemplating what was on the other side. Iona joined them.

The view through the window was murky: it was

darker on the other side than it was out here. She might be able to see more if she got closer to the window (it had no shutters and unlike normal windows there was a flat, transparent sheet that filled it and formed a barrier, stopping you from reaching inside), but nobody ever liked to get too close. The only thing she could see clearly was the figure standing on the other side, staring back at her.

Nobody knew how many figures there were but people had reported seeing as many as four at once. They were gray, ugly things, their bodies uneven and untidy. Their eyes were huge and black. Their shape was similar to that of a normal person but their form was entirely other. Many people found the sight of them too disturbing and never came out here to look, but others liked to watch them, consider what they might be and what their presence might mean. Some people came out here to ask questions of the figures, looking to them for a sort of spiritual guidance, and sometimes even claimed to have heard an answer. Iona came from time to time, usually when she was feeling troubled. Not because she hoped the figures would give her the answers to her problems but because seeing them put her problems into perspective. They were an unknowable element of the world. Anything Iona was going through seemed simpler by contrast with trying to understand the figures.

At least, this was usually true. But now she found that

however long she looked at the figure, the incident at the funeral refused to sink back in her mind.

After a while Iona realized she would be late for her afternoon class if she didn't set off for the school now. She kept turning back as she walked away but the figure was still there. Eventually the window was obscured by the trees.

The sounds of the city returned to her ears. Iona wondered if the figure had ever heard them.

The king received the long rolled-up sheet of paper from his attendant and said, "Thank you," but didn't mean it. He found something inherently unsatisfying about looking at plans, they just made him want to see the actual finished thing. Also the technical detail went right over his head. But this design had been delayed in its progress through the various preapproval stages and the architect had an appointment at planning tomorrow to receive feedback, so he couldn't put it off.

But first he was going to eat his dinner, so he sent the attendant away. Dinner tonight was a bland vegetable stew and flatbread. The food wasn't enjoyable, but then food wasn't something you enjoyed. It was something you did alone, quickly, before anyone saw. Even Clarence left him alone when he ate.

The king wondered what other people ate. Was his food particularly fine or was it the same stuff everyone else had? He didn't know. Nobody ever talked about food and if he raised the subject people would lose respect for him.

The king finished his food and returned to the plans. He unrolled the paper and laid it on the table by the window. The paper rolled itself back up. He searched vainly for something heavy enough to keep the paper in place—a book perhaps, or a cup—but he couldn't find anything. His attendants had tidied everything away.

He could call them back. But he was fed up with people doing stuff for him. He wanted to sort this out for himself.

The king removed his shoes and placed one on the middle of either end of the paper; this worked except now the corners rolled inward. He moved his shoes into the top corners and held the bottom corners flat with his hands. This was better. He could see the plans properly now.

But he couldn't pick up his pencil, which lay on the windowsill. He needed his pencil to make notes on the plans. But if he let go of the plans they'd roll up again.

"Bugger," said the king.

Then Clarence leaped up onto the table and sat on one

corner of the paper, freeing up one of the king's hands. The king used the free hand to pick up his pencil.

"Thanks, Clarence," said the king.

"Not at all, Your Highness," purred Clarence.

The king tapped the pencil against his teeth as he cast his eye over the plans, which were for a new forestry office building. The architect had coped with the limited space available by designing the building in a shape akin to a neat, evenly spaced cluster of trees. The building stood on a series of sturdy "trunks," three stories high, each of which contained a stairwell: on the top of each trunk was mounted a hexagonal polygon containing a further six stories. This had the appearance of a very stylized mass of foliage. The polygons were linked by walkways. Yet as well as having an original, apt, and even witty design, the building was also practical—the upper floors would receive a lot of natural light, the lack of which was an increasing problem in the more built-up areas of the city. The lower floors, which would be quite dark, were to be used for filing and so on.

The king was much impressed, and said so.

"It *is* good," Clarence agreed.

"It's amazing," said the king. It was so good it overcame his usual antipathy toward looking at plans. "We don't have anything like it. I love it. I'll be able to see it from my window, won't I?"

"It should be bigger."

The king glanced back at the drawings. "It's already bigger than the old forestry office."

"But it'll fill up in no time."

"You think?"

"Of course," said Clarence, and rattled off a few statistics about the rate of employment at the bureau, which the king had no intention of checking. Clarence had a good memory for that sort of detail and the king relied on him to get such things right.

As usual the king was torn between wanting a city that worked for the people who lived here, with enough space and facilities for everyone, and getting the place finished. The city's needs kept growing in spite of his efforts to keep it stable. It seemed there was nothing anyone could do about this.

Eventually the king was convinced by Clarence's argument that a bigger building would be more future-proofed—they didn't want to have to knock it down in a few years and start again because the city had outgrown it. The king picked up a pencil and located the space on the edge of the paper that had been left blank for his notes. He scribbled *Looks awesome, pls make bigger, great work,* and then a smiley face. Clarence jumped off the table and the king removed his shoes and put them back on his feet. The paper rolled back up of its own accord and the king left it on the table for his attendants to collect and take back down to planning.

———————

Alyssa arrived late for their first tutorial, apologizing and claiming to have gotten lost on the way. She was not wearing the hat, although she was wearing a long, thick coat that seemed quite unnecessary for the weather today.

"You can hang up your coat over there." Iona pointed to the ornately carved hat stand next to the door.

Alyssa glanced at the hat stand, then turned back to Iona. "I'm fine. I'll keep it on. Can we start?" She seemed on edge. She was looking around a lot, and kept glancing over Iona's shoulder to the window.

Iona was a little uneasy herself. The hat may have been absent but Alyssa's appearance, her manner, her speech—all of them were strange in a way Iona still couldn't put her finger on.

Yet Iona had kept the appointment. So maybe she *wanted* to put her finger on it.

Iona started to outline what she was going to cover in this first session—a heavily condensed version of a ten-session first-term course on foundations she had taught more times than she could count, covering principles, methods, and common difficulties. Then she stopped and asked Alyssa if she was following along so far, because the young woman was giving her a blank stare.

"Actually," said Alyssa, "I was going to ask if maybe you could show me a real one?"

Iona blinked. "A real one?"

"Yes. Like a real building site? I think I'll learn much better that way, instead of just talking about it in this small office."

———

Out in the city, downtime had begun. The manufacturing plants lay silent: so did the building sites, except for one or two where work had fallen behind schedule. The streets were quiet. Iona could hear chatter from residential buildings where citizens had gathered in pairs to talk, and realized that giving Alyssa this tutorial was perhaps the closest she had come to doing the same. This realization emboldened her to broach the subject that had been bothering her.

"Did you hear about what happened at the funeral yesterday?"

Alyssa looked up sharply. "What? No. There were lots of funerals yesterday, which one?"

"He was called Weston. My colleague."

"No."

"It was very strange," Iona said, and described the event.

Alyssa listened and nodded, her gaze fixed on the ground. "Yes, strange," she agreed when Iona had finished, then she looked up and said, "Wow, that's an amazing building." She was talking about the old sawmill. Back when this was built the forest had only been a stone's throw from the center and the city had only been the town. The old sawmill was used purely for fine-cutting work these days: large-scale wood processing happened at the newer, larger mills. The building was the shape of an incomplete sphere set into the ground, with large open areas to let in the light. Its imposing shape bulged outward and then swept back like a wave before connecting with the ground again on the other side. The interior, most of which was visible from the outside, was functional and unprepossessing—but this made for a smart aesthetic contrast between the shell and the contents.

Iona stopped walking and followed Alyssa's gaze. "You must have seen it before, surely." It was a bit hidden away these days—a number of tall blocks had been built around it and the path that led to it, once a major thoroughfare, was now a back alley—but everyone surely passed it at some point.

"Of course," said Alyssa after a short pause, and then hurriedly added, "I'm just looking at it with fresh eyes because we're talking about architecture and stuff."

"I thought you were thinking about tearing it down."

Alyssa spun around. "Me?"

"I mean 'you' as in the planning department. I thought they recommended it should come down to make way for a residential block."

"Oh. I don't know." She looked back at the building. "Did *you* design it?"

Iona was about to say yes, but then she doubted herself. "I, er . . ." She *thought* she had. She certainly felt that connection she felt with all buildings she'd designed. But now that she thought about, it surely the building was too old to be one of hers? And she couldn't actually remember designing it.

But then she remembered the textbook. It was used in there as a demonstration of the techniques that held the roof in place, and all the examples in the textbook were drawn from her own work.

"Yes," she told Alyssa. "I did."

"Wow, you're *really* good."

Iona laughed. "How gratifying."

"Oh, they *can't* tear this down, it's lovely."

Iona shrugged. "One can't be too sentimental." Many times she'd seen her creations torn down, broken up, consigned to the furnace, and the energy sent back into the city. Each time she had turned away and set to work on something new. "For me the satisfaction lies in having done the work, not in having it stand there until the end of days."

"That would do my head in."

"Every building falls down eventually."

Together they walked on.

―――――――――

They arrived at the new housing estate that was being built at the city limits. A few months ago this had been part of the forest, but at the most recent cull it had not been replanted and a new area farther out had been seeded in its place. The layout of the new estate resembled a spoked wheel, with six streets leading off from the center. Backing onto each row of houses was a community garden. The wheel motif was to be replicated in the detailing on the houses. As yet, however, the builders hadn't gotten past the foundations. Which was why Iona had brought Alyssa here.

Iona ducked under the hazard tape, taking care not to tear it, and walked to the foundations of the nearest house.

"It is, er . . . alright for us to be here, isn't it?" Alyssa said, tentatively following her.

"Why do you ask?"

"Just because of how it's all cordoned off . . ."

"Oh yes, as long as you're with me it'll be fine." Where architectural business was concerned she was allowed everywhere as long as she didn't get in the way.

A ladder was propped against the side of the foundations and Iona used it to climb down to below ground level. Alyssa held the ladder steady, then joined her.

"So what are we looking at?" Alyssa said, shoving her hands in her pockets. Alyssa's hands were constantly in her pockets.

Iona directed Alyssa's attention toward the walls that had been built up around the edges of the hole they currently stood in. She showed Alyssa how they were layered and linked, and explained how the boards had been treated to prevent warping as they absorbed moisture from the soil. A stack of fresh boards lay to one side, ready to be put into place tomorrow: Iona picked up one of the shorter boards and pointed out how it had been cut to interlock with the others. "The important thing is to ensure these holes line up," she said, pointing at a large square hole, "because there's a locking support beam to slide through that, which will hold them together and form the skeleton of the walls aboveground."

Alyssa nodded. "And you always make them out of wood?"

Iona peered at Alyssa. "What else would they be made of?"

Alyssa stared back at her for a moment. "Yes, of course. Silly question. Anyway, this was really helpful." She turned to go back to the ladder—but Iona put a hand on her shoulder.

"No, you must have been thinking of something else. Tell me."

"Ignore me, you know far more about these things than I do—"

"Tell me," said Iona with more force than she'd intended. But she desperately wanted to know what was on Alyssa's mind. Because it was true, the wood warped so easily, there had to be something better than wood but what could that be? She was thinking of the hat, the *felt* hat, and she felt sure Alyssa was about to say—

"Stone?" Alyssa said, looking anxious.

Iona shook her head. "Stone is too precious, the quantities are too small, we need it for furnaces, and—that's not what you were going to say. What were you going to say?" She tried to be less intense, make it sound like more of an academic interest. "Good ideas can come from anywhere, I just wanted to listen to your—"

"I was going to say . . . concrete."

Concrete. It was a dream-word. Somehow Iona knew Alyssa was about to say a dream-word. Even stranger than that was how the dream-word seemed to fit perfectly in the conversation when, by rights, it should make no sense at all.

"What *is* concrete?" Iona asked.

"Don't you know?"

"Just tell me."

"It's . . . just something I heard someone say. I don't know what it is. I shouldn't have mentioned it. Tell me more about foundations. It's fascinating."

Iona felt sure Alyssa was lying, that she knew what concrete was but didn't want to say. Did Alyssa have the dreams too?

3

"OUCH!" SAID THE KING.

Clarence trotted into the king's chambers with a noticeable lack of urgency. "What's the matter?"

The king leaned over and showed Clarence his thumb. A splinter protruded from the center of a tiny but growing bead of blood.

"Are you expecting me to pull it out?" asked Clarence.

"No, I can do that myself. You asked me what the matter was so I showed you." The king turned away and walked to the window to get better light. He plucked the splinter out, flicked it away through the window, and sucked on the wound.

"How did it happen?" asked Clarence. "Was it the wall again?"

"No, my crown." The king's crown lay on the floor, where he had dropped it due to the shock. "I'm sending it back. It's not properly finished. The inside rim isn't smooth enough. That could have gone right into my head."

"Imagine the carnage. Are you going to have anyone punished for it?"

"What? No." The king sucked his thumb again. "When have I ever had anyone punished for anything?"

"If you did, maybe it would raise standards."

"I'm not going to."

Clarence sighed. "You always want people to *like* you."

"Yeah," the king replied, sitting down in his chair by the window. "Of course I do. Doesn't everyone?"

"Sometimes a leader has to make difficult decisions. Decisions that might be unpopular."

The king thought for a moment. "Don't think I have."

"In which case you've been fortunate."

"Or maybe this city's just very well run, eh?" And with that the king opened the newspaper. It was a good edition. Lots of coverage of the funerals, and there was a long article about a day in the life of a materials courier. He read the entire paper from front to back, then went back and skimmed it again. He asked Clarence if previous editions of the newspaper were stored anywhere.

"No, Your Highness," Clarence replied.

"Really?"

"Yes, really. Why?"

The king shook the newspaper. "The whole history of the city is in these."

"The history is all in the public records—"

"But that's just old maps and planning decisions—I'm

talking about *this*." The king turned the newspaper to the article about the courier. "Stories about real people and how they lived—people are more important than buildings. There's so much that no one will know about if we don't keep these. Right, that's it—we're starting a newspaper archive."

"We'd need a lot of space—"

"We've *got* a lot of space. What's the problem? You don't usually need convincing about new building projects."

"No, but we already have so many construction sites in operation—"

The king snapped his fingers. "I know—they're building new offices for the newspaper, right?"

"Well . . . yes, but it's been delayed by—"

"Yeah, yeah, I know—but they *are* moving out of the old offices. So when they move into the new place, the old offices can be the archives."

"Well . . . if you're sure—"

"I am. I think it's a good idea." The king held up today's edition. "And we can start with this one."

———

"Sorry, are you busy?" asked Carter as he entered Iona's office to find her with an exercise book open on her desk and two piles of similar books on either side of it.

"Just marking," Iona replied. But the truth was she had not done any marking for several minutes. Instead she had been staring at the open book while replaying last night's conversation with Alyssa in her head; thinking ahead to their session tonight; and writing the word *concrete* on a piece of scrap paper, wondering if she had spelled it correctly. Without drawing undue attention Iona reached out, screwed up the scrap paper, and tossed it in her wastebasket.

"This'll only take a moment and then I'll get out of your hair," said Carter, placing a copy of this week's newspaper on her desk. "Have you seen it yet?"

"Seen what?" Iona peered at the front page, which featured a report from Weston's funeral. Initially she assumed it had made the front page because of the strange events at the end but she quickly realized the report made no mention of this at all. The funeral was the lead story purely because of Weston's public standing and the circumstances of his death, and although it was a nice gesture the result was a completely uneventful piece of writing.

"Gosh, how bizarre," Iona said, "they haven't mentioned the disturbance *at all*. Why act like it didn't happen?" *Finally,* she thought, *someone to talk to about this.*

"Oh—I don't know," said Carter. "Actually that's not

why I brought it to you." He opened the newspaper and showed her the king's column, which took up the entire third page. This week it was all about Weston and his contribution to the city.

"Right," said Iona, embarrassed to have raised the matter of the disturbance. It seemed Carter wanted to act like it didn't happen too. "How nice."

"Yes, but look." Carter pointed to the fourth paragraph.

Iona peered at it and saw her own name amidst a block quote from the eulogy she'd given at Weston's funeral. "Oh." She picked up the paper, sat back, and read the text. Rather embarrassing that she'd thought these words wouldn't be recorded at all, and here they were in the king's column. She wondered who'd passed this on to him, since he hadn't been there himself.

When she was dead, who would speak at her funeral? Would the king write a column about her too? It felt terribly vain to think of it but then she'd designed more buildings than Weston. She'd designed more buildings than anyone.

Iona held up the newspaper. "Thank you for bringing this—may I borrow it?"

"Keep it," said Carter, heading back to the door. "I've finished with it."

————————

During her midday break Iona locked her office while she ate lunch and read the newspaper. In the column the king admitted he had only met Weston a couple of times at opening ceremonies, but had been struck by the outpouring of public feeling upon his death. After some quotes from tributes, the king went on to praise Weston's contribution to the city and called him a model for his fellow citizens.

It occurred to Iona that it was odd she had never met the king. Yes, he was an important man and the demands on his time must be considerable, but Iona's work was closely linked with government and she could certainly consider herself a public figure, if only a minor one. It was surprising their paths had never crossed. All her designs were signed off by the king—she had a meeting at planning later today to receive his feedback on her latest—so he must at least be familiar with who she was, surely? Or maybe he didn't pay attention to such things.

Well, if the king didn't know her name before, he certainly knew it now.

Iona wondered how long people would remember her for. While her buildings still stood? How long would they stand? What would replace them?

She put the brakes on this self-indulgent train of

thought. She leafed through the rest of the newspaper, which was mostly filled with building reports and consultation debates as usual. Usually she would recycle the newspaper at this point but instead she put it in her desk drawer. It was something nice to remember Weston by.

————————

"Well," said the chap at the planning department, whose name was Rankin, as he unrolled the plans. He was new—Iona didn't remember meeting him before—and seemed slightly overwhelmed by the scale of the latest round of projects, including the one they were here to discuss.

Iona's proposed design for the new forestry office was one of the most ambitious she had ever submitted, but she had not created it out of hubris. Rather, her intention had been to fit a large building into an already crowded part of town while causing the least possible upheaval. Her innovative concept meant that an adjacent residential block could be preserved, so there would be no need to turf people out of their homes and move them to one of the new estates in the suburbs.

"We're all very impressed," said Rankin, clamping the plans to the display board behind him. "Everyone's very excited about the design. Very excited."

"Great."

"We all love what you've done. It's so bold."

"I'm glad."

"The king especially. He was knocked out when he saw it."

"Gosh."

"He did have just one note for you."

Iona nodded. "Sure. What?"

"He'd like it to be bigger."

Iona looked from Rankin to the plans and back again. "Bigger in what way?"

"Just generally bigger. I think it's a mark of how excited he is about it."

"Well—" Iona began. "Do you mean taller?"

Now came Rankin's turn to glance at the plans. "Yes. Well. He didn't say."

"Broader? More capacity?"

"Um . . ."

"All of those things?"

"*Yes.* All of them. I haven't spoken to him personally, you understand."

"No."

"I don't enjoy that honor. But he wrote this on the edge." Rankin pointed at the king's scrawled note on the corner of the plans. Iona stood, walked over to the board, and squinted at the comment. Indeed, that was the king's sole instruction: the building should be bigger. And then there was a smiley face.

Iona straightened up. "Well, making it taller, with this design, putting more weight on the struts . . . I'm not sure it would work. I don't think it'd be safe."

"Oh."

"So we'd have to make the whole thing broader as well, but—"

"Excellent. Do that then."

"But that would mean thicker struts, so you'd be looking at extending the whole thing down this side." Iona ran her finger along one edge of the diagram.

"We can accommodate that. The king is keen to accelerate the building program."

"Oh good," Iona said, although she couldn't remember a time when they hadn't been accelerating the building program. "But what about the residential block?"

"That's alright, we'll demolish it."

"Right. I did sort of design the whole thing so that wouldn't be necessary. That was the whole idea."

"That's really considerate of you," said Rankin without any sarcasm at all. "But we don't mind. It's quite old anyway."

———

After the meeting Iona returned to her office to wait for Alyssa, although she was by no means certain she would turn up. They'd parted ways last night on an uneasy note and maybe Iona had scared her off. Iona felt surprised by how keen she was to see and speak to Alyssa again. The young woman understood nothing about architecture but Iona felt increasingly certain she understood other things.

Iona's intention had been to finish the marking she'd started earlier, but as she sat down she noted another colleague had left a copy of the newspaper on her desk, presumably unaware she'd already seen it. She was about to toss it in the wastebasket but stopped herself and opened it instead. She stared at the third page, reading the king's column again, lingering over that fourth paragraph. It was strange to think of the king knowing who she was, because she had always felt like she knew him. But probably everyone felt like that.

Alyssa entered the office without knocking and Iona hastily set aside the newspaper. "Sorry, got lost again. I read what you said about your friend," Alyssa said, her manner easy and open and betraying none of the edginess of last night. "It was lovely." She didn't sit down. "While I was busy getting lost I had an idea of where we could go today, if you don't mind."

———————

Iona hadn't intended every tutorial to take the form of a field trip but she was amenable to whatever Alyssa wanted to do. She was thinking less about the content of the tutorials and more about using this time to puzzle Alyssa out.

Together they walked to a half-completed building, the skeleton of which reached a height of eight stories. The ground floor was much taller than the rest and had been designed to accommodate printing presses. The floors above it had been intended as offices. An ornate entranceway gave access to both spaces—you could either take the stairs up to the offices or walk through to the print shop floor. However, the site had been emptied of all tools and materials and cordoned off with a temporary fence. This was because the entire structure listed 9 degrees to the right and 5 degrees forward. Part of the building had collapsed and supports had been put up. The rubble of the collapsed section had been cleared away. The sign on the fence read UNSTABLE—KEEP OUT.

This was going to be the new newspaper offices. Iona had been surprised when Alyssa had suggested coming here—the young woman had asked if she felt okay about it. But Iona gave it some thought and decided it would do her good to see.

Iona stepped over to the fence and found a plank that hadn't been properly fixed into the ground, betraying the speed with which the fence had been erected. She lifted the plank aside, making a gap large enough to squeeze through. "Come on," she said to Alyssa.

Alyssa glanced around herself, then followed Iona inside.

Together they proceeded around the perimeter between the fence and the building. "Mind your head," Iona said as they reached the corner, where the building's tilt was at its most extreme and the gap between building and fence was narrowest. When they reached the right-hand side of the building Iona crouched down and indicated where the wall had fractured. "So you read the report about the collapse in the newspaper?"

"Yes."

"Then you'll already know what caused this."

"I've forgotten. Subsidence?"

"No, the ground underneath was solid. The foundations were prepared in the same way as the ones I showed you yesterday."

"Were they not slotted together properly?"

"No—there was a mistake when the boards were being cut. The wood had been incorrectly loaded so the grain was pointing the wrong way and the boards were weak. The central support beam of this wall tore straight through them." Iona straightened up. "Nine people were killed."

"Including your colleague."

"Yes," said Iona. Weston had been on-site, consulting on modifications to the design, when the collapse had occurred. It could easily have been her standing by that wall.

Mistakes happened. She made plenty herself. She didn't feel angry at whoever had made this one. But she hoped they were not in a position to repeat it. There were plenty of other jobs they could be moved to.

"So what are they going to do about it?" asked Alyssa.

"They're building a support structure for this wall and then they'll finish the building. They'll be able to publish three editions of the newspaper a week when it's done." Although she wasn't sure what would fill those extra editions, since a bigger building didn't mean there was more news to report.

"And they're just going to finish it to the original design? Even though it was dangerous?"

"It won't be dangerous, we know what the problem was. I think the feeling is it would be a fitting tribute to Weston to complete his design as he intended."

"So this was all him? You weren't involved?"

"No."

"But you've designed more buildings in the city than anyone else."

"I haven't counted." But it was true. She didn't need to count.

"You've been doing it longer than anyone else, haven't you?"

Iona hesitated. "I *have* been doing it a long time . . ."

"But when did you start?"

"Why do you want to know?"

Alyssa gave her a relaxed smile and shrugged. Her hands were in the pockets of her coat again. "I'm just interested. I thought it'd be a simple question."

Iona nodded slowly. "It should be a simple question. But I don't know." She tried to think back—when had she started doing this? What did she do before?—but all she found inside herself was a rising sense of panic. Focusing on the question was like staring at the sun—no, the opposite. It was like staring into the void, like facing an awful truth she couldn't bear to acknowledge, that she could only cope with by looking away. She felt nauseous and dizzy, and involuntarily put a hand on Alyssa's shoulder to steady herself. The younger woman flinched.

"Are you alright?" Alyssa asked.

"Yes," said Iona. "I'm tired. Can we finish this tomorrow?"

"Do you need me to walk you home?"

Iona shook her head. She was already making her way back to the gap in the fence. "I'll catch a rickshaw."

"Do you want me to come with you?"

"I'll be fine."

———

Iona told the rickshaw driver to go slowly because she was feeling unwell. She was afraid she might throw up, and the thought of people seeing the contents of her stomach made her feel even worse. The driver was quite old anyway, and not capable of pulling her very fast even if he wanted to, and they completed the journey without incident.

Iona entered her house and went to bed even though it wasn't yet late. She lay there and wondered if she really wanted to finish the tutorial tomorrow. Perhaps she'd followed her curiosity about Alyssa too readily. Their first two meetings had made her uneasy but the experience she'd just had at the newspaper office had terrified her. She should have heeded her sense of unease, not rushed toward the source of it.

Before drifting off to sleep Iona resolved that tomorrow morning she would write to the planning department and, with apologies, tell Alyssa she was busy with design projects and would have to discontinue the tutorials.

———————

The king's attendants came to wake him in the middle of the night. He didn't come around right away, so Clarence jumped on his head to speed the process along.

"What is it?" the king asked.

"Open the window and see for yourself," Clarence replied.

The king got out of bed, taking the blankets with him because it was cold. He pulled open the shutters—

And smoke poured in. Masses of it drifting right toward the tower. The king blinked it away and tried to see where it was coming from.

Through the murk he could see a building below blazing from the inside, the flames licking around the windows and threatening to spread to the exterior at any moment. He was unsure which building it was. The smoke made everything look different.

"Oh my *god*!" said the king, his pulse rapidly rising. "What are we doing about it?"

"Don't worry, the firemen are already there."

"Right. Good." But the king didn't feel reassured at all. He squinted to try and see the firemen. It was just as well the city *had* some firemen, even if he couldn't remember the last time they'd been needed. "How did it happen?"

"We'll have to find that out."

4

THE FIRST IONA KNEW of it was as she crossed the street to go to work. A newspaper distributor was handing out a new edition, which struck Iona as odd because there had been an edition published only yesterday. Sometimes if an issue was in heavy demand it would be reprinted the next day: had the report on Weston prompted this? The urgency of the clamor around the distributor suggested otherwise. This was not a crowd gathered for yesterday's news.

Iona walked over to the distributor and took a closer look at his wares. Indeed, the newspaper was a new edition. Iona held out her hand, accepted a copy, and read the news.

Her immediate reaction to learning of the fire was sadness and pity.

Then she realized which building had burned down, and her next reaction was panic and paranoia.

Upon entering the school Iona strode directly to her office, closed the door, and locked it. She went over the events of last night in her mind. She had told nobody they were going to the construction site. Alyssa said she'd had the idea about going there on the way to her office, so it was unlikely she had told anyone. And they hadn't actually gone inside the unfinished newspaper offices, and it said in the report that the fire had started inside the building. Iona was feeling so guilty she had to remind herself that she *had not* started the fire. She and Alyssa had left the building exactly as they'd found it.

But they *had* gone into the building site last night. Had anyone seen them do that? From a window across the street perhaps? If so, Iona could truthfully say she hadn't gone into the building itself but nobody would have reason to believe that. Had the rickshaw driver realized where she'd just come from? Iona didn't think so—she'd hailed him from around the corner—but maybe when he heard about the fire he'd put two and two together?

And was Iona certain Alyssa had nothing to do with this? Could Alyssa have tossed something inside while Iona wasn't looking? Left something burning so slowly it didn't catch until they'd gone?

Iona had a choice. She could come forward and tell the Bureau of Order she'd been there last night. If Alyssa was involved in what had happened, Iona would be helping bring her to justice. Iona was innocent so she had nothing to fear.

Or did she? Nobody knew why she had associated with Alyssa. Only the two of them knew why they had gone to that building. If Alyssa chose to bring Iona down with her, she could easily name Iona as her accomplice, claim they'd planned it together. And even if she didn't, people might say Iona had helped her unwittingly and was a fool for doing so. People might judge Iona a liability, decide she should have asked more questions and next time the consequences could be more serious. She might be punished. Stripped of her position. Retired in disgrace.

She would say nothing.

———

Unfortunately, nobody in the staff room talked of anything else.

Had the fire been an accident? Or had it been started deliberately? Either way, would it happen again? Who could have done something like this, and why? Iona had none of the answers and didn't want to give anything away by speculating. She just said she felt bad about the waste of materials and labor.

"Yes," said Hammond, a senior member of the teaching staff. "But we can't rest easy until we find out who did this." He theorized that it might have been burned in protest at the deaths of Weston and the others: because they wanted more severe punishment for those responsible, or were outraged the building wasn't going to be abandoned, or both.

"That's assuming the fire really was set deliberately," Iona replied, trying to sound uninterested.

Hammond leaned in toward her. "You and I both know it was."

Iona blinked. "Why do you say that?"

"Because we've studied how fires start. Even accidental fires are caused by people. Something poorly maintained, or left burning when it should have been put out. But nobody had been in that building since the collapse. Why would it suddenly burn down now?"

"I suppose you're right," Iona admitted. She had been deluding herself with the possibility that the authorities would conclude it was nobody's fault and ask no further questions. "But then," Iona continued, "it might be a blessing in disguise."

Hammond looked at her quizzically, and Iona instantly regretted having said it.

"I just mean it was going to be such a lot of work to repair the damage," she went on, "and would people ever have felt comfortable in it? I'm just thinking of the people who would've had to work there. We can start afresh and do it right."

"That's not like you. You love solving problems."

"Maybe I'm just getting old. Don't have the energy to think my way around things anymore."

"As you said before though, such *waste*. If we'd made the decision to tear the thing down, it could've gone into the furnace. But all that heat, just going into the air . . . awful. How much power could that have generated?"

Iona said she'd love to stay and help him work it out, but she had to go and teach her morning class.

───────────

A heavy, dismal feeling washed over Iona when she realized her students also wanted to talk about the fire.

She tried to start the lesson but the students were utterly preoccupied. She deflected the issue by turning the lesson into one about how good design could help prevent fires, and demonstrated how the layout of the city had stopped yesterday's fire spreading to other buildings. This held her pupils' interest sufficiently that they stopped discussing why the fire had started.

Afterward Iona returned to the sanctuary of her office and sat behind the desk. She considered closing the shutters so no one could see her but realized this would look strange. She would sit here and do some work, or at least give the appearance of doing some work. She found the pile of marking she had set aside yesterday. It all seemed so long ago and she struggled to find where she'd gotten up to with it. Finally she settled, opened an exercise book, and tried to focus.

She had done barely anything when the knock came at her door.

They could have sent a message. She would have come willingly if summoned. But, Iona realized as the officers marched her through the corridors, she had brought this on herself by not coming forward voluntarily. They were punishing her for that. If she had gone to them herself it could all have been done discreetly. Nobody need ever have known.

Now everybody would know. Staff and students lined the corridors, stepping aside to allow her to leave, their own business suspended, the atmosphere strange. She wondered how much they knew. If there was anything they didn't know, rumors would fill the vacuum.

As she walked out of the school doors and began the journey to the Bureau of Order, a small crowd of familiar faces watched her go. What did they think of these events? As usual, Iona had very little idea what other people thought.

———————

Iona had designed the bureau herself. A broad, four-story cylinder of a building, like a pillar with nothing to support, it lay in the shadow of King's Tower. The rooms at the center had no windows. This was to permit discussions of a sensitive nature to take place. As Iona was in one of those rooms now, she presumed she was about to take part in a discussion of a sensitive nature.

Iona sat at the table in the center of the room. The room was lit only by a fire at one side, the heat from which was captured and put to work elsewhere in the building. But not *all* the heat could be captured and there was enough left over to make the room uncomfortably warm. This was deliberate—she had been asked to design it this way. Iona removed her jacket and hung it on the back of the chair.

A guard stood at the door. This seemed unnecessary. Why would she escape? Where would she hide?

The door opened and in walked a woman in her fifties with close-cropped black hair, a hawk-like face, and black clothes. She was a little taller than Iona. Iona didn't recall having met this woman before, but then she'd had very little contact with the bureau beyond designing their offices. Was she in charge here?

The woman carried a briefcase that she placed on the table as she sat down opposite Iona. She opened the case and brought out paper and a pencil. Some of the sheets of paper had already been written on.

"Your name please," she said, looking at the paper, not at Iona.

"Iona Taylor."

The woman wrote this down.

"And you are?" Iona asked.

"We've met before."

"But you asked my name."

"Because that's procedure."

"Right. Well, I'm afraid I don't remember yours."

"Saori Kagawa. I'm head of operations."

"This is about the fire, isn't it?"

"Of course."

Iona wondered whether the head of operations was tackling this personally because the case was particularly important or because the bureau had nothing better to do. There was rarely any trouble in the city—she couldn't recall the last time she'd read about any in the newspaper. (Although she remembered how the newspaper had not reported the incident at Weston's funeral.)

"What do you want to know?" said Iona.

"I'm afraid we didn't bring you in for your expertise, Ms. Taylor."

Iona swallowed, inwardly saying good-bye to her faint hope that they *had* brought her in for her expertise. At this point she should probably admit she had been to the site of the fire just hours before it started. But what good would it do her now?

Saori shifted uncomfortably in her chair. "There's no easy way to say this . . . There's a detail of the investigation we haven't released to the public. We've been sifting through the remains of the burned building—and we found a body."

Iona inhaled deeply. It would be Alyssa. Someone had seen them together and the bureau wanted to know what their connection was. Perhaps they wanted her to identify the body.

"It's your colleague," said Saori. "Weston."

Iona blinked. "But he's dead."

"I know he's dead—as I say, we found his body, or what was left of it."

"No, I mean he died *before* the fire—"

"To be strictly accurate his *funeral* was before the fire, but these new events have cast doubt on whether he *died* before the fire. That's why I called you in."

Iona took a moment to comprehend what Saori was

implying. "He died in the accident—it was all in the newspaper—"

Saori looked down at her notes. "You're sure he was dead at the funeral?"

"I saw him in the casket—"

"And you're sure it was him?"

"Of course—" Iona paused, remembering what had gone through her mind briefly at the funeral—how Weston didn't quite look like himself. But it had been such a nebulous, easily dismissed feeling. It *had* been him lying there. "It was definitely him," she said.

"You had to think about it."

"I didn't *have* to think about it, I wanted to."

Saori nodded. "Did you witness the incident at the end of the funeral?"

Iona tensed up even more. Did they know she'd tried to speak to others about the incident?

"Yes . . ."

"Describe it to me, please."

"One of the mourners stood up, ran down the aisle, and jumped on top of the coffin."

"Do you know who he was?"

"No, do you?"

"Was the coffin open or closed?"

"Closed."

"What happened next?"

"Well, the coffin went into the furnace."

"With him on it?"

"Yes."

"Do you have any idea why he did that?"

"Nobody did. I think it was the oddest thing any of us had ever seen."

"In your view," said Saori, interlacing her fingers and leaning forward, "is it possible he could have gotten the coffin open and removed Weston from it—"

"While they were in the furnace? No."

"You seem sure of that."

"Both of them would have been overcome by the heat and smoke within seconds."

"But you couldn't see inside."

"No, the door to the furnace was closed."

"Then you can't be sure."

Iona was about to give a snappish response to this but stopped herself. "I worked on the design for that building. I know the layout. The coffin hits the flames as soon as it's inside. When the main doors close the heat is intense—and the only way out would be through the stoking hole at the far end. There's no way a person could cross the flames and get there alive."

Saori nodded and made a note. "That's very useful insight, thank you. Weston also worked on the design for that building, didn't he?"

"Yes. But what does that have to do with—"

Saori shrugged. "I just find it interesting."

"You're suggesting he used that knowledge to escape from the furnace?"

"I'm not suggesting anything, I'm merely gathering facts—and somehow I have to reconcile what I've been told about the funeral with the fact his charred body was pulled out of the remains of the newspaper office. Which I understand he *also* designed. And which is where the accident that allegedly killed him occurred."

The way Saori had just arranged the facts made it sound like Weston had come back from the dead and taken fiery revenge on the building that killed him. But Iona wasn't going to comment on this, because it was insane. Instead she leaned forward and said, "He *was* dead at the funeral, though. So why would someone steal his body and then put it in a building they were going to burn down? It doesn't make any sense."

"I agree. Be grateful you're not the one who has to make sense of it."

———

When Iona returned to the school nobody asked her where she'd been or why they'd taken her away. Nobody spoke to her at all. They just spoke to each other in low voices as she passed them in the corridors. She wasn't sure what to say: she wanted to assure people she wasn't a suspect but she also didn't want to spread these bizarre ideas about Weston.

Iona went back to her office, sat down, and quietly finished the pile of marking that still lay on her desk. Shortly after laying the final exercise book aside she heard a knock at the door.

"Come in," she said, reluctantly.

Carter opened the door and hesitated on the threshold. "Are you—?"

"It's fine. Come in."

Carter closed the door and sat down opposite. "I took your afternoon class. I'm afraid nobody else was available."

"Good. Thank you."

"I had your lesson plan to follow, which made everything very easy."

"Teaching's not hard if the students are good."

"They are good students."

Here the platitudes ran out.

"They wanted to ask me about the fire," said Iona.

"But nobody thinks . . . I mean, you didn't—"

"No, it's—it's Weston."

"What?"

"Don't tell anyone, please."

"Of course, but what do you mean—"

"His body was found at the site of the fire."

"Which . . . is the place where he died."

Iona nodded.

"But we *saw* his body go into the—"

"Yes, I know and I told them that. They had some idea that the mad fellow at the funeral smuggled his body out—"

"That's impossible too."

"I know. I don't pretend to understand it at all."

"So they brought you in—"

"Because I knew him and we designed the Point together. So they asked how sure I was that he was dead, could he have faked it . . ."

"Gosh. Glad you're in the clear, anyway."

The phrase *in the clear* resonated with Iona. She had a vision of a clear space, where she could breathe and move. She did not feel in the clear right now.

It was almost the end of the school day when Carter left, but Iona stayed in her office anyway, pretending to work, waiting until the building was empty so she could leave without having to talk to anyone.

Only when she was preparing to go home did it occur to

Iona that Alyssa was supposed to be here right now for another tutorial. This morning Iona had been torn on whether or not to send that message over to the planning department telling her not to come. She wasn't sure which would draw more attention to the connection between them—sending the message, or not sending the message and having Alyssa turn up here. She'd come to no conclusions and after the interview at the bureau she'd forgotten about it entirely. But Alyssa hadn't turned up anyway. Iona wondered where she was.

The king had spent much of his day at the window looking down at the blackened hole that had been punched into the surface of his city. The investigation team from the bureau was examining the site, looking for evidence. The king wished they'd hurry up so the cleaners could come and sweep it away.

The king dreamed of the day when the city was finished. He wanted to look out from his windows onto an unblemished view, with everything looking as it had been designed to look, and he could feel satisfied at having overseen it, and the citizens would be happy with what he'd done for them. He tolerated the constant presence of building sites across the landscape because they were stages toward achieving this aim. But looking out on the remains of a destroyed building upset him deeply. Everyone else talked about catching who was responsible, and that was fine and important, but the king would rather be talking about what they were going to put in that blackened hole. Would they start again using the same plans, finish the newspaper offices as originally intended? Or should they come up with a new design, push themselves to put an even better and *bigger* building in that space? He was anxious for these questions to be settled, and for the answers to not derail his plans for a newspaper archive. He was very keen on that.

The king had been called away from the window a few times for consultations and updates, but kept returning to fixate on the scorch mark on his landscape. In the late afternoon he had gone to his armchair to rest. Overwrought and emotionally exhausted, he'd fallen asleep.

When he awoke the room was dark: one of his attendants must have come in and closed the shutters. The king stood and marched to the window, hoping the day he'd just experienced had been a dream.

He opened the shutters: the building was still gone. Of course it was.

Clarence trotted in, carrying a letter. He dropped it onto the floor and said, "Ah, you're awake."

"Yeah, sorry, I fell asleep," the king replied, closing the

shutters and turning away from the window.

"Don't apologize, it's been a long day."

"So what else has happened?" The king yawned. "What's going on?"

Clarence tapped the letter with his paw.

The king peered at it. "But we've already had the letter today."

"This is an update."

"Do we need an update?"

"We thought you'd like one."

The king picked up the letter, opened it, and paced the room while he skimmed its contents. He was breaking his own rule of reading letters methodically from front to back, but this one didn't follow the usual format—it was devoted to a bureau report on the investigation. They'd questioned some people, they had some suspects—they'd found a body. They were certain the fire had been started deliberately.

That part terrified him. Deliberately? Why? He couldn't imagine what would motivate someone to do that. He felt personally offended. He provided these buildings for the citizens—it was an act of love. And for this gift to be not only refused, but *obliterated* . . .

The final pages terrified him more. The bureau had speculated on the potential for a recurrence of the incident. The possibility that the culprit might strike again, or that the same urge might exist in others. The bureau believed the possibility was high.

"So it could happen again, then," the king said, the pages of the letter quivering in his hands. "What do we do?"

"We stop them," Clarence replied firmly.

"Yeah. I mean we know everyone in the city, don't we? So we must be able to work out who did it."

"Exactly. And the whole city is keeping an eye out for this kind of suspicious behavior now."

"Yeah." The king looked back down at the letter. "Says here there's another special edition of the newspaper tomorrow to keep everyone informed." Ironically they had never needed a bigger newspaper office more than they did now. "Have I got time to do a column?"

"Yes, if it goes off tonight."

The king nodded. "I think I should. Everyone will want to know we're on the case with this. Something with a big headline, 'My Promise to You,' by the king: your safety is my priority, et cetera."

"Do you want to write it now?"

"Er . . ." The king closed his eyes and pinched the bridge of his nose, then he shook his head. "I'm still tired. Could you write it for me?"

"If you like."

"You know what sort of thing I want to say, don't you?

I'm just—I need some rest." The king snapped his fingers and an attendant came to help him get changed for bed. The king looked down at the nightclothes the attendant held.

"I'm not due for new pajamas, am I?" he asked.

"Your old ones smelled of smoke, sir," said the attendant. "I recycled them."

"Oh. Good." The king finished dressing. "Help Clarence write my column, would you?"

The attendant nodded and left, Clarence trotting after him. "Sleep well," Clarence said as the attendant closed the door.

But the king did not sleep well. He dreamed of the tower burning down around him. Every wall was ablaze and there was no way out.

5

IONA WOKE UP TOO early and couldn't get back to sleep. She got up and ate breakfast, as always, with the shutters closed. But even when she finished breakfast she didn't open them. Today she wanted to be alone with her thoughts.

She had made a decision never to tell anyone about her tangential part in the arson incident. That was straightforward enough but she was thinking over the ramifications. Even if her secret was never discovered, merely having it separated her from everyone else and it always would. She felt like she had wandered a little farther from home than usual, only for the ground to crack behind her and a tectonic shift to pull her away.

Tectonic was another dream-word. She grasped its meaning but it related to nothing in the real world. These words seeped into her internal monologue quite often, never to be used in conversation. When she spoke aloud she found other words.

Nobody knows how strange I really am, thought Iona.

She finished eating, walked the short distance to work,

and went directly to the chancellor's office. She told the chancellor that Weston's death had hit her harder than expected and she'd like to take a few more days off. Her request was accepted. Her requests were always accepted.

Upon leaving the school grounds she walked down to the site of the fire, telling herself there was nothing suspicious in this—lots of people were going there and unlike them she could pass it off as professional interest. Of course she couldn't get very close: the investigation was still ongoing and a high fence had been hastily erected around the ashes and charred fragments. There were several gaps in the fence and citizens gathered around them to peer morbidly in. Iona stood at the back of one such crowd and waited for those in front of her to drift away.

When she got her turn at the front there was little to see. The blackened frame of the unfinished building was being dismantled before it fell down and the job was almost complete. A deconstruction team carefully lowered beams and struts to the ground and gathered them in a stack, ready for the furnaces to extract any remaining energy they had to offer. Other workmen filled cart after cart with ash and towed it away to the landfill.

At the foot of the fence people had laid flowers even though the official story was that nobody had been inside the building when it went up. What they mourned was the building, like it was a newborn child that had never gotten out of the hospital. (Dream-words again.)

Iona looked up from the flowers. A few meters away on the other side of the fence, watching her, stood Saori.

Iona met her gaze and nodded, as she would to a colleague in the corridor at the school. After a moment Saori nodded back.

———————

The facts were these: Iona could not tell Saori or anyone else at the bureau about Alyssa, not without incriminating herself. She was also worried that if the bureau's suspicion did turn on Alyssa, then Alyssa might very well tell them about her association with Iona. But at the moment the bureau seemed to be occupied with investigating Weston. Which gave Iona a chance to track Alyssa down and get some answers for herself.

To this end Iona arrived at the planning department and went to the front desk. The young woman behind it was called Quinn.

"Hello," said Iona. "I'm looking for someone called Alyssa who works here? Where's her office?"

Quinn looked puzzled. "I don't know the name..." She reached for the staff directory and started looking through the entries. "How are you spelling that?"

Iona wasn't entirely sure—she'd never seen it written

down—but gave it her best guess.

"And you're sure she's in planning?" asked Quinn.

Iona was not sure. Alyssa might have been lying to her. But for Quinn's benefit she said, "I'm *fairly* sure . . ."

Quinn kept on looking through the directory, shaking her head. "Sorry. She might be new? This thing isn't always up to date. If anyone knows, it'll be Victor."

Iona thanked the young woman for her help and walked up to Victor's office. She'd had a little contact with Victor—he worked on planning policy and made recommendations to the king, so Iona had read various proposal documents he'd written. He was also responsible for assigning staff to the various planning teams, so he knew everyone who worked here.

His office was at the top of the building. There was a desk just outside the office door, which was presumably where his secretary worked, but the desk was vacant right now so Iona knocked on the door herself. There was no response. Presumably Victor was in a meeting somewhere. Iona had time on her hands and no other leads on Alyssa's whereabouts, so she decided to go into the office and wait for him.

Victor's office was on the side of the building that faced away from King's Tower and had once offered an excellent, 180-degree view across half the city, but the view was now partly blocked by the buildings that had risen around it. Victor's job meant he needed a good view from his office for reasons beyond his own aesthetic pleasure, so Iona had made sure to provide him with one in the new planning office. Perhaps that was where he was right now, preparing for the big move.

Iona walked over to the window behind Victor's chair. She ought to be able to see the site of the fire from here. The sun was bright and as she moved into the light she flinched away from it, looking down—

And it was then that Iona saw something glinting between the floorboards. The sunlight was catching it in an unusual way. She kneeled down. The glinting came from an object that was wedged between the boards. With the aid of a pencil she pried it out and held it in the palm of her outstretched hand. She barely had any time to consider what the object might possibly be before Victor's secretary came in and found her kneeling behind the desk.

"What are you doing here?" said Victor's secretary, whose name was Lewis.

As Iona stood up she unobtrusively slipped the object into her jacket pocket. "Waiting for Victor," she said as innocently as she could manage.

"He's not here."

"I realized. When will he be back?"

"He . . . hasn't come in for two days."

"Is he unwell?"

"We don't know. He . . . we haven't heard from him."

This was intriguing.

"What did you want to talk to him about?" said Lewis. "I might be able to help."

"I'm looking for someone and I think she works here. Her name's Alyssa?"

"No, there's no Alyssa here," said Lewis—but then a thought seemed to strike him and he held up a finger. "Hang on." He left the office and returned to his desk. Iona followed him: he was opening a large-format notebook. At the top of each page a date was marked. It was a diary.

Lewis found the page with today's date. It listed all the day's meetings. They had all been neatly crossed out, a single ruled line obliterating the text. Lewis turned back one page—the days immediately before were the same, all crossed out. Iona counted back the days. There were seven days on which everything had been crossed out. Victor hadn't been in for two days but he'd been canceling all his meetings for five days before that.

Lewis turned back a couple more pages, stopped, and ran his finger down a page. He tapped a line near the bottom of the page where something had been belatedly squeezed in, a single word: ALYSSA. Next to it was a time, right at the end of the working day.

"So he met her?"

"Seems like it."

"Do you remember her?"

"Sorry—a lot of people pass through this office."

"Thank you," said Iona and left.

———————

The morning wore on but still the king lay in bed. He had woken up early with bad dreams, but instead of getting up he lay there, thinking.

Clarence entered, carrying the morning letter. He stopped and dropped the letter onto the floor.

"I'll read it later," the king said, without turning over.

"You should stay up to speed," Clarence replied.

"I'm sure they're on top of it. What do I even do anyway? I said the other day that I never made any tough decisions—but I never make *any* decisions."

"Nonsense. Only last week you decided on the design for the new street maintenance building."

"From a choice of two. Either of which would have been fine."

Clarence trotted to the side of the bed. "Come on. Rise and shine."

"I'm trying to get some peace and quiet, Clarence."

"Your city *needs* you, you can't just lie in bed—"

Clarence bent down, clamped the bedsheets between his teeth, and pulled. The king gripped the sheets and pulled back. The sheets tore down the middle, forcing the king to get out of bed and seek some clothes.

"The city needs me to do *what*?" said the king furiously as he searched for some underpants. "I stay up here all day, I only really talk to you and these guys—" Here the king indicated one of his attendants, who had just arrived with his trousers. "I read all about people's lives but am I *connected* to them? I bet to them I just seem distant, like I don't care—"

"No no no. You're the heart and soul of this city."

The king chose some shoes from a selection of three proffered by the attendant, then turned back to Clarence. "You say that but this fire business—what if people feel like I'm not listening to them and they have to burn down a building to get me to listen? What if next—"

"With respect, you're flattering yourself that *everything* is about you—"

"Let me finish," snapped the king. "What if next time they burn down *this* place?"

"The tower is much, *much* better guarded than an empty, unfinished building—this is the safest place you could possibly be."

The king was staring out of the window, shaking his head. "I've been up here too long."

"Focusing on the reasons for this attack endorses destruction as a means of—"

But the king was already walking toward the door.

Clarence hurried around in front of the king, alarmed. "Your Highness, you can't—" he said, but the king just stepped over him.

"You can come with me if you like," said the king as he left his chambers.

Clarence had no choice but to follow.

———

Iona sat at the table in her house, spinning the object she had found in Victor's office. She did this by grasping the object with her left thumb and right forefinger and flipping each side of the object in a different direction simultaneously. She watched it spin for a few moments, then slapped her hand down to stop it. She didn't know how she knew how to do this, because she had never seen anything like it before. But she had done it without thinking.

The thing was made of metal, so first of all it was odd to find it lying around. Metal was a precious commodity in the city and was only used where there was no adequate substitute. It was used for cutting-tools, for example, and in larger furnaces such as the ones in the Points of Return (domestic furnaces were generally made of stone). This small disc served no such purpose.

Despite all this Iona knew what it was. Her first sight of the object had prompted the dream-word *coin* to spring to the front of her mind. Another word had followed it: *money*. It was a unit of common exchange. You earned it with labor and bought things with it.

But money was not a concept that existed in the real world. In the city you weren't paid for your work and if you wanted or needed something you just asked for it. So why was this here?

Iona picked up the coin. It was very weathered and a small hole had been drilled into it just inside the edge. She let it tumble down the outside of her fist. She didn't know how she'd thought of the trick but she mastered it very quickly. As if she'd done it before.

Iona was coming to the conclusion that these were not just things from her dreams but things she had forgotten, and that made her wonder why she hadn't seen them in so long.

It was quiet on the street where Victor lived. This was a district for high-ranking professionals and they weren't around at this time of day. Iona found Victor's house (she noted with amusement it was another of her designs) and knocked on the door.

There was no answer, but Iona was in no hurry. She knocked three more times, leaving a minute or so between each knock. While she waited she looked around, checking who might see her. Victor's house had an extensive porch that partly hid her from view.

When Iona felt sure nobody was watching, she pushed the door. It opened—doors in the city only locked from the inside, so that appeared to confirm Victor wasn't at home. She stepped into the house and closed the door behind herself.

Iona searched through each room. The house was neatly kept, not dissimilar to her own. The main point of difference was that at the back of the house he had a small workshop with a fine set of tools, a workbench, and some good-quality wood. The workshop was lined with shelves containing a number of small carved ornaments, presumably made by Victor himself. The pieces were crude, lacking the finishing that the city's manufacturing plants offered—definitely the work of an amateur, though they were much better than anything Iona could muster.

The piece on the workbench attracted her attention.

It consisted of a cylinder about thirty centimeters long, slightly tapered and with a larger cone on the tapered end. Two holes had been drilled in the cylinder and a couple of slim, short rods had been slotted in. These rods had rectangular panels attached to them. Iona moved her hands closer to the object but stopped short of touching it. She knew the object was very important but she also felt afraid.

Iona took the object and turned it over in her hands. It had been sitting upside down on the bench but Iona didn't know how she knew it was upside down. The rectangular panels were adjustable and she tilted them forward and back.

A name appeared in Iona's mind: *Mull of Kintyre.*

Now Iona imagined the same shape, but not made of wood: she imagined it in black and gray and white, and made from materials whose names she couldn't think of right now. She saw it on a huge platform in a place with no trees or buildings. She saw herself, and some other people, going inside it . . . but she couldn't imagine why she was going inside it and she couldn't picture the faces of the people who were with her. But she felt sure this was a model of something larger . . . something that really existed somewhere.

But where though? You couldn't hide something that size in this city. And why had she forgotten about it for so long?

Iona had to stop looking at it now because she was in danger of being overwhelmed by the thoughts it was triggering. She went to search the rest of the house.

The idea had been for the king to see what people's ordinary, everyday lives were like but, as Clarence pointed out, there was a paradox at the heart of this, because as soon as people saw him they stopped their ordinary, everyday lives to gawk at him.

"But I want people to see I'm just a normal guy really," said the king.

"What a ridiculous thing to say," Clarence replied.

"I am though. I never asked to be king, did I?" As he said this the king wondered if that was actually true. He couldn't remember if he'd asked or not. But it was true he was just a normal guy. He was an amiable sort of bloke who just wanted people to think well of him and for everyone to get along. No drama.

Clarence leaped up onto a fence and hissed in the king's ear. "People don't want to think you're normal. They need a focal point—someone they can look to for a leader."

"How do you know what they want? Have you asked them?"

"You're not helping anything here. We should be going about things as usual, not changing your routine. Whoever started the fire probably *wants* us to worry and panic."

"Who's worrying and panicking? I'm just going for a walk."

And the king kept walking.

———————

On the upper floor of Victor's house Iona looked through his small collection of books but this was more out of prurient interest than anything else—she always liked looking through other people's books. He seemed to enjoy escapist fiction.

Finally she looked in the bedroom. This was a personal space and she'd left it until last because she was undecided whether to go in there at all. But the carving told her she needed to know more about Victor. If he had made that he could explain to her what it was and why she remembered it.

The bed was neatly made and did not look slept in. There were still clothes in the wardrobe—she wondered if he had taken any with him at all. Next to the bed was a chest of drawers. She opened the top drawer.

Inside she found a single folded piece of paper. She unfolded it.

The paper had been printed with a series of diagrams:

she quickly realized these were stages in a process. It was an instruction manual, and Iona wondered what for. As she stared, she eventually perceived something in the simplified shapes in each diagram—but she still didn't understand what these instructions were telling her to do. She turned the paper this way and that and concluded she was still missing something.

But still, the paper piqued her curiosity. She put it in her pocket and left the house.

———————

The king had almost reached the edge of the city, where it wasn't so busy. Citizens who weren't at work—seated in pairs at tables—looked at him through their windows and he waved cheerfully to them. A small crowd had been following him at a short distance all the way from the city center. They were a bit weird but their presence cheered him, just knowing they cared enough to follow him around. He couldn't see Clarence but assumed he was somewhere in the crowd.

The king paused and wondered where to go next. He decided he'd walk around the city limits for a while and then head back into the center via a different route so he could see some other parts of the city. The little crowd moved after him.

Until now the king had been enjoying being out in the city, getting a feel for the rhythms of ordinary life. But as he looked through another window and saw another pair of citizens sitting at a table, something troubled him. The silence of the suburbs troubled him. The idea of what the city would be like after that longed-for day of completion troubled him.

He felt like he was missing something very important.

Then one member of the small crowd broke away from the rest and raced toward the king, who failed to react before the man clubbed him over the head with a mallet, beating him to the ground.

6

AS IONA PASSED PEOPLE in the street on her way home she vaguely noticed they seemed troubled, panicky even—something had happened and it was causing alarm. But she was too preoccupied with her own thoughts to ask about it, or even to speculate. Maybe another building had burned down. She felt surprised by how little she cared. Right now all she cared about was getting home. She hurried along, avoiding eye contact with everyone she passed.

Iona entered her house, closed the door, and put the instruction manual she'd stolen from Victor's home on her table. She unfolded and flattened it and studied the steps again, over and over. She spent a long time doing this—she lost track of how long. Slowly it became clear what they were telling her to do. It seemed insane yet the bright, clear presentation was so lucid, professional, official—boring, almost.

She wondered if she had the nerve to carry out the instructions.

A knock resounded through Iona's house. Nervously

she hid the manual in a kitchen cupboard, then she went to answer the door.

————

The king woke up, remembered what had happened, and cried out in alarm.

"Calm down, Your Highness," said an attendant—a rather shapely female one. She laid a hand on his shoulder and gently eased him back down into his bed.

Bed. He was in bed, and everything was fine, and his shutters were closed, and nobody was trying to attack him. Still, he started in surprise when Clarence jumped onto the bed.

"How are you feeling?" asked Clarence.

"How do you think I'm feeling?" said the king. "Someone hit me on the head with a bloody *mallet*."

"I *did* advise you against going outside."

"*You* told me the citizens love me!" The king put a hand to his head and for the first time registered the presence of a bandage. He winced.

"Your Highness, there's always *some* discontent—but it cannot be cured by going among the people. You merely put yourself at risk."

"Why is *anyone* discontented? We give them everything they need. Everyone's got a job, everyone's got a home—what else am I supposed to do?"

"It's not always enough to make people happy."

"So who was he? The guy who did it?"

"His name was Ward. But don't worry, he's dead."

"Good." The king said this a little too vehemently and it made his head ache again. "Who killed him?"

"Your loyal subjects took revenge on your behalf. Which is technically murder but—"

"Yeah, I'll overlook it."

"So you see, most people *do* love you. They rushed to your aid. It's only a small minority who—"

Clarence was interrupted by a knock at the door.

"Tell whoever it is to go away," sighed the king.

"I don't advise that," said Clarence.

"You're full of advice today—*why* don't you advise that?"

"She's a reporter from the newspaper. She wants to interview you about the attack."

"Oh." The king sat up in his bed. "Fair enough, I'll talk to her then."

The reporter was a young earnest type, clearly a little overwhelmed to find herself in his presence. The king gave her some good material about how his visit had stirred his pride in the city—even the attack, because the people had shown loyalty and courage in defending their king. He encouraged her to speak to the people who had rushed to his aid, get them to tell her their stories.

"That was very good," said Clarence after the reporter had left.

"I thought so," said the king.

"You should get some rest."

"Yeah, that has taken it out of me a bit." The king returned to his bed, went back to sleep, and dreamed of pushing the man who'd attacked him into a furnace.

———

Carter had come to see how Iona was. Which was nice of him, she kept telling herself: he'd obviously heard she'd asked for time off for personal reasons. But she was nervous and distracted and knew she was coming across as such.

"What have you been doing with yourself?" Carter asked. Iona realized they were sitting at her table opposite each other, just as she'd seen other citizens do many times through the years but never done herself. What a strange time for this to happen. She wanted to enjoy it—but she kept thinking about the diagrams. Her mind kept superimposing them on Carter because that was, inescapably, what they showed: the body of a person.

"This and that," said Iona. "I did mean to take some proper time off but I've got design work with deadlines."

"Good chance to catch up on it, I suppose."

"Yes, I've . . . got some modifications to make to the forestry office design."

"Has anything else happened with the investigation?"

"I was going to ask *you* that. I haven't heard anything at all. Are they still going on with this theory about Weston?"

"I don't know. You're the only person who's mentioned it."

Silence fell. Perhaps Iona could just tell Carter what she'd found, show him the coin and the manual. The young man had an inquiring mind. They could discover the truth together. But with a queasy feeling Iona realized there was another opportunity here, one she couldn't pass up—she was alone with another citizen in the privacy of her house, someone who trusted her and deferred to her seniority. It was an ideal chance to test what she'd seen in the diagram.

As she debated it in her mind she realized she was going to do it and the longer she left it the harder it would be.

"Would you like to hang your jacket up?" she said to Carter. "You must be warm."

"Oh," Carter said. "I wasn't going to stay long—"

"Have you got something to get back for?"

"Not exactly, but—"

Iona stood. "Come on. Give me your jacket and we'll have a chat. I'm thinking of writing a paper on planning regulations, maybe you could help."

"Alright," said Carter after an uncertain pause.

Iona tried to swallow down the tension in her throat.

Carter leaned forward and removed his jacket.

Iona walked swiftly around to the back of Carter's chair, gripped his shirt with both hands, and lifted it to reveal what lay underneath. There she saw exactly what the diagrams had depicted—a hatch in Carter's back, about a foot square—and in that moment she knew everything in the diagrams was true. But she couldn't ponder this discovery just yet.

"What are you doing?" asked Carter, giving Iona no time to think about what she was looking at—she had to act. As per the instructions she pushed on both top corners of the hatch simultaneously and the hatch fell open.

Carter stopped. That was the only way she could describe it—he simply stopped. He didn't move or speak or display any awareness of anything.

Iona walked back around to the other side of the chair, still expecting Carter to move at any moment. Her colleague sat motionless, jacket dangling from his fingers. Iona carefully extracted the jacket and hung it on the back of her own chair, then she sat back down and faced Carter again.

Carter stared back at Iona. But he didn't, Iona now realized, because Carter had no eyes—his head was contoured to suggest eyes but there were no eyeballs or sockets. Neither did he have a nose or ears. A slit was positioned where the mouth should be but it was a crude rendition of a mouth, narrow and almost rectangular. Carter's features were smoothed over, like a dummy's head.

Iona moved her chair closer and hesitantly touched Carter's face. Carter didn't react. Iona traced the contours of his head. It remained entirely immobile. It was carved from a single piece of wood.

During their acquaintance Iona was sure she had seen Carter smile, frown, sniff, raise his eyebrows—and yet she was looking into a face that could do none of these things. Had it changed when she'd opened the hatch? No, Iona realized—it was just that she was seeing him differently now that he'd stopped moving. His movements had been so human, his manner so real, she'd assumed he was a human being and some part of her mind had filled in the details, stopped her from seeing his real face. This was the face Carter had always had and she'd simply never noticed—had never really looked at him properly. Like a building you walk past every day and you think you know what the upper floors look like, then one day you actually look up and they're completely different.

If Carter was not, in fact, a human being—what was he?

Carter's wooden head sat on wooden shoulders, which in turn supported articulated wooden arms and sat atop a wooden torso. Iona examined Carter's hands, noting that—unlike the head—each was made up of at least twenty discrete moving wooden parts. It was a very fine piece of mechanical engineering.

Iona glanced around the room and suddenly became very aware of her open windows. Hoping nobody had seen anything untoward, she made a quick circuit and closed every shutter. Then she walked to the front door, locked it, went to the kitchen, retrieved the instruction manual, and returned to Carter. She had completed the first step and with some trepidation she supposed she should proceed with the rest. She walked around Carter's chair again, leaned over, and peered at what lay inside the hatch: could it really be as the diagrams depicted?

It was. Carter's body was occupied by machinery—all made of wood. Cogs, pistons, and dozens of tiny switches. The wood was warm with recent activity and gave off a rich smell but the workings lay still. There was a clockwork mechanism that presumably powered them. She reached a hand up to her own back but felt nothing similar there. Her skin was unbroken.

Iona consulted the instructions again. One of the diagrams was headed MOTION TEST and an arrow indicated one of the switches. Iona reached her hand inside, suppressing a churn of revulsion, and flicked the switch.

Carter jolted and Iona jumped back, grazing her hand on the edge of the hatchway as she pulled it clear of the workings. Carter rose from the chair, stepped clear of it, and turned a full circle on the spot. Iona panicked, her mind racing through apologies and cover stories, until she realized Carter wasn't conscious. This was a purely mechanical operation with no intelligence guiding it. Carter flexed his arms, raised his legs high, and moved his head from side to side and up and down, performing what looked like an obscure military drill. Inside the cavity in Carter's back the cogs and pistons were in motion. Then he sat back down and returned exactly to his starting position, his hand positioned as if still holding his jacket.

Startled, Iona waited a moment to ensure Carter had finished moving. Then she returned to the cavity in his back and consulted the instructions again. Another diagram was labeled VOICE TEST and an arrow indicated another switch. Iona operated it, noting how clean the switch felt under her fingers: these had rarely been used, if at all. Iona felt glad she didn't have to look into Carter's face while this happened: what she was doing felt sickeningly intimate, performed without consent.

A sound emitted from the slit in Carter's face. Iona recognized the sound as his voice but, as with the face, she realized she'd perceived it inaccurately until now. It didn't sound as smooth as she'd thought: it had a broken, slightly harsh quality. "Voice test in progress," Carter said, then he recited the first few lines of *Kubla Khan* by Samuel Taylor Coleridge (a poem that was familiar to Iona even though she couldn't think where she might have heard it before). As Iona listened to the texture of the voice she thought she detected something percussive. The diagram indicated a sliding switch labeled PITCH. Iona reached around, slid the switch downward, and listened as Carter's voice deepened and slowed. Iona slowed it right down to the point where the voice was exposed as being made up from a series of incredibly rapid taps or clicks, the binary pattern of noise and silence building into more complex shapes.

The slow sound unsettled Iona and she slid the switch back up. However, the voice was higher and faster than Carter's ought to be. Iona moved it down a little—and now found it too low. Her pulse suddenly rose, her hands trembling as she tried to locate the switch's original setting, desperate to undo her meddling. The more she listened to the voice in subtle variations, the less she felt able to recall Carter's true voice. Eventually she settled on something that sounded more or less right, but would other people notice if it was a little bit off? Would Carter notice if his voice was not quite his own?

The next diagram was headed PERSONALITY SETTINGS. Iona did not dare touch any of these but in case she did so accidentally, she fetched a pencil and on the back of the diagram she made a note of all the positions. There were perhaps fifty switches covering the personality functions. On the diagram they were labeled things like CHARM, STABILITY, MELANCHOLY, HUMOR, INTENSITY and each had a range of four settings. How much variation could be created with these simple controls? How many different personalities? The permutations were not infinite but the city could go through many, many generations before it had to start repeating the patterns.

The penultimate diagram had been annotated by hand. A series of switches at the bottom was marked with numbers 1 to 9 and then 0, and next to this was a long code. Iona guessed perhaps this was some security code to confirm her interference was authorized, and had to be input before closing the hatch? Whatever it was, it was part of the sequence and it seemed wise to carry it out.

The code contained over fifty digits and the switches were small and fiddly. When pressed, they made a *click* and then slid back into position of their own accord. Iona entered the code steadily, ticking off each number on the sheet as she went to ensure she made no mistakes. Finally she pressed a switch marked ENTER at the end of a row, and as instructed by the final diagram, closed the hatch.

Abruptly Carter stood and marched toward the door. Iona was startled and blurted, "Wait!" but he ignored her. No—it was as if he hadn't heard her at all. He lifted the latch on her front door and walked outside.

Iona didn't know what to do. Was Carter going to tell someone what had happened here? She had to make him listen—assure him she'd meant no harm by it. But right now he was walking away. She stepped outside, closed her door, and ran after him.

———

Iona caught up with Carter as he strode down the street away from her house. She fell into stride alongside him and spoke his name in a low voice but again, it was as if he had not heard.

"Where are you going?" said Iona.

Carter said nothing and kept walking.

Iona looked around. Nobody was nearby, so she quickened her pace and stood in front of Carter, blocking his path.

Without missing a beat Carter took a step to his left, walked round Iona, and kept going. He hadn't reacted like you would to a person being in your way—it was like he was walking around a pillar.

Iona followed, this time a few steps behind so she could observe him. He walked at a constant, brisk pace and stared straight ahead. When he reached the end of the street he turned neatly on his heel, faced right, and walked down the next street. He seemed to be going somewhere and it wasn't his home, or the school, or even the bureau: if he was going to any of those places he'd have turned the other way at the junction. And wherever he was going, he wasn't speaking to anyone or looking at anything on the way.

Iona wanted to know where he was going and the only way to find out was to keep following.

———

The king rolled over to find Clarence sitting on his pillow. "There's a rumor going around that you're dead," the cat said.

The king blinked. "Okay, tell them I'm not."

"They're gathering outside the tower and demanding to see you."

"But look what happened last time I went outside."

"I'm not suggesting you go outside—just go downstairs and wave at the window."

"But what if someone gets a bow and arrow and shoots me?"

"We're policing the crowd. If anyone's got weapons we'll pick them up."

"How big's the crowd?"

"A hundred, maybe two."

"Ohh . . . I don't know about this."

"People have to know you're not dead—it'll only cause more unrest if—"

"Alright, alright." The king got out of bed and looked for some trousers. He couldn't wait until they caught the people who were causing all this chaos and things finally got back to normal.

———————

Carter attracted no attention from other pedestrians. To them he just looked like another person going about his business. And he did look like just another person, Iona noted: it wasn't just Carter she'd perceived wrongly all these years—it was everyone. Her fellow citizens might all be different heights and builds, with their own distinct body language, but they were beings made of wood like Carter and they always had been. The engineering of their bodies was precise and elegant but the face had been left out entirely, as if that level of subtlety was not even worth attempting. Perhaps blankness left more space for the observer to read their own meaning into it—after all, this was exactly what Iona had done. Their expressions were entirely suggested by their movements and tone of voice, and her own imagination filled whatever gap remained.

But how *could* she have not seen? Did she simply see what she wanted to see? She looked down at her own body, spreading her fingers, expecting the illusion of flesh to fall away and be replaced by wood: but nothing changed. She was different from the others. Perhaps she'd wanted to believe she lived among her own kind and her perceptions had obliged. Or perhaps it was a trick she had only now seen through. Whatever it was she could not unsee it. The action of opening Carter's hatch had broken the spell. Everywhere she looked she was surrounded by wooden automata and it was all she could do not to panic.

She focused on the simple task of following Carter. He led her past buildings she had designed. Rows and rows of houses. Machines for living in. Machines for machines to live in.

They were in the suburbs now, in places Iona had rarely visited since construction there had been completed. Iona had to keep pace with Carter but as she passed close to an apartment block she peered in the windows. Every apartment had an identical table and chairs in the center of the living room and every table had two citizens sitting at it, facing each other, unmoving. Every apartment.

———————

As they reached the edge of the city Iona noted a street corner in the suburbs had been cordoned off. The bureau was investigating a crime here. Usually anyone passing a crime scene would look up, at least to register that it was there, but Carter continued to stare straight ahead.

They walked on, left the city behind, went into the woods. Iona had always seen the trees as raw material for the next house, office, public facility, etc. Now inside each one she saw a person waiting to be carved out. The forest seemed a vast, silent womb, its unwitting children vested with infinite patience.

Eventually Iona and Carter reached the mouth of a disused mine shaft. It had been decommissioned several years ago because of concerns it might cause subsidence under the suburbs if it was extended farther. Surrounding the shaft were the traces of foundations where the site offices had once stood—when the mine closed down they had been broken up and sent to the furnace. The city never let a building stand empty when its materials could be put to good use elsewhere.

Carter didn't stop at the mouth of the mine shaft—he just walked inside and started to descend. Iona hesitated. Going into the old mine shaft was forbidden, although the penalties for trespassing were not explicit. The fact it was known to be unstable was enough to put most people off. But Iona had to know why Carter had come here. So she followed him down.

The air inside the mine was dank, the ground moist. Rain would run down here and take a long time to disperse. Iona was accustomed to having the hearty smell of clean-cut wood around her. Down here she could taste only decay.

More pressingly, the inside of the mine was dark and Iona had no source of light. When the mine was in use the struts that supported the roof would have had torches attached to them but these had long since been removed. Before long it would be impossible for her to see anything. She was faced with a decision and had barely any time to make it: if she turned back toward the entrance now she would lose Carter and never find out why he'd come here. Maybe there was no logic, maybe he was leading her to nowhere—but instinct told her there was a purpose.

As the light dwindled Iona put her hand on Carter's shoulder before she lost sight of him. He didn't react, just kept walking—and she let him lead her farther and farther into the darkness. She swallowed down the fear that she would never get out again and hoped that when Carter stopped walking this would all make sense.

Iona's thoughts and fears were interrupted by splitting pain as she walked into something, cutting her forehead in the process. She put out a hand to touch whatever it was.

There was a wall ahead of her, and it wasn't made of soil or wood. It wasn't quite metal either. It was hard and smooth—a little like the wall at the edge of the forest. But it was *underground.*

Iona heard a movement from nearby. She wondered if it was Carter—in the last few moments she had lost track of where he was. "Who's that?" she said—but she received no answer.

A knife was held to her throat.

———

Fresh rumors washed from one side of the crowd to another. There was nothing malicious in these rumors. Nobody here wanted to get rid of the king. The rumors were driven by uncertainty, verging on panic. New editions of the newspaper were being printed as fast as details could be confirmed, in an effort to calm the populace—but these were just words on a page. Could they be trusted? If the king could be attacked in public, who knew what to trust anymore? Were they foolish even to trust each other?

More than once a hush came over the crowd as they anticipated the king's arrival, but when he didn't appear the murmurs would start again and then build. Who had said he would be here anyway? Perhaps that was just another rumor? What would they do if they didn't get to see him?

Then a figure appeared at the window. It was not the king but an attendant in household uniform. He signaled for silence and got it.

And the king appeared. He smiled and waved to his people. He didn't even look that badly hurt.

The crowd cheered and applauded.

Up at the window the king allowed the sound of their adulation to wash over him. He found something oppressive about the noise, even if it was well meant. His concerns over his personal safety were replaced by a deeper unease. All he'd ever wanted was for the citizens to be happy and to like him, and now he feared his relationship to them had changed forever.

He wondered how much longer he needed to stand here.

7

SOMEONE SWITCHED ON A LIGHT, so that was something at least, even if the knife was still threatening to slice open Iona's windpipe. The light shone directly into her eyes and obliterated everything else in her vision. Its source was a handheld torch. (Not fire, Iona thought: *electricity.* Another dream-word with newfound purpose.) The hand that held it did not belong to the person who held the knife: the holder of the knife was behind her, the holder of the torch was in front.

"It's her," said the holder of the torch. "The architect." Iona recognized the voice as Alyssa's and found she wasn't surprised. If anyone had an electric torch, *of course* it would be Alyssa.

"What's she doing here?" said the holder of the knife, who was a man. "Did you tell her—"

"No," said Alyssa. "She doesn't know anything." Alyssa raised the torch a little, shining it toward the ceiling so its light was no longer in Iona's eyes. "How did you find us?"

"I followed Carter," said Iona. Her eyes were adjusting to the darkness and she could see Alyssa was standing in a doorway, just to the side of the wall she'd walked into. Carter must have gone through that doorway.

"Who's Carter?" said the man with the knife.

"A colleague of mine—look, do you really think I'm a threat?"

"What do you reckon?" the man said to Alyssa.

Alyssa peered at Iona. "I don't think so."

The man lowered the knife and walked around to join Alyssa, and Iona now saw he was Victor—a slightly built man in his early forties, darker-skinned than herself, whose default expression was a scowl. But most significantly both he and Alyssa were real people like herself, not things made of wood. Iona realized this with relief—she was not the only one. Perhaps they could help her understand.

"Why did Carter come here?" asked Victor.

"I don't know," said Iona.

"Are others coming?" said Alyssa.

"I don't think so." She felt it was important to tell them the truth about everything so she told them how she'd set out to find Alyssa, which had led her to the planning department, which had led her to Victor's office. She took the coin from her pocket and held it up.

"Oh *that's* where it went," said Alyssa, smiling broadly and taking the coin from her.

"It's yours?"

"It was part of my charm bracelet," Alyssa said, holding up her wrist with the bracelet on it that Iona had found distracting on their first meeting. "Thank you—I was gutted that a piece had gone missing. It's not the same without all the pieces."

Iona went on to explain how the absence of Victor at his office had led her to visit his house. Victor was furious with Iona over this. Alyssa was furious with Victor for leaving the instruction manual lying around for people to find.

"I left in a hurry," Victor said. "I didn't get a chance to go home and tidy up—and I didn't think anyone would go snooping in my stuff." This last part was directed more at Iona.

"And you carried out the instructions on this citizen, this Carter?" said Alyssa.

"Yes. I wanted to know where he was going so I followed him—why did he come here?"

"The instructions are for testing new citizens after they're assembled," said Victor. "I added the last part myself—it's a simple program that tells them to come here and wait."

If that was simple, Iona wondered what a complex program would look like. But instead she asked a more pressing question: "Why?"

"Because we need them," said Alyssa. "Why were you looking for me?"

Iona remembered she had reasons of her own to be angry with Alyssa. "Because they questioned *me* about the building that burned down, the one that you and I had been to a few hours earlier, and the bureau thinks my friend faked his own death to do it, and I'm sure you must be involved in all this and I want to know how."

"But you didn't tell the bureau you were there, right?" said Victor urgently.

"No, I didn't want them to know I had any connection to it at all."

Victor turned to Alyssa. "What do you think?"

Alyssa considered for a moment. "I think she's telling the truth." She gestured to Iona. "Come inside."

Iona looked up, unsure what it was she was being invited inside—but as Alyssa's torch flashed around, she realized her surroundings were as familiar as her own shoes.

"The *Mull of Kintyre*," she breathed.

———

The king had returned to bed. One of his attendants had brought the newspaper for him so he could read how his assault had been reported. The article's description wasn't quite as he remembered it but then again he'd suffered a significant brain trauma, so maybe the report was right and his memory was wrong. He'd barely gotten a glimpse of his attacker and couldn't now picture him at all—the man's face was a blank in his mind. There were also several details the king hadn't told the reporter and he wondered where those had come from. Probably Clarence had filled those in.

On the second page was an article about Ward, his attacker. This explained more about who he was and speculated on why he had done it. Ward had been a construction worker, passed over for a teaching post several times. His colleagues noted he'd been struggling with physical tasks and speculated he might have a repetitive strain injury. Perhaps he had feared retirement. Perhaps that was why he wanted that teaching job so much. Perhaps he could see no way out. But, as his neighbors were quoted as saying, nobody had suspected he would do something like this.

The king thought about his attacker for a while.

After some consideration he called all his attendants. He would need them.

———————

Iona felt queasy to be walking once more along the corridors of the *Mull of Kintyre.* Alyssa led the way through the ruined spaceship. Iona noticed parts of the interior had been dismantled—whole rooms were missing—and she wondered aloud why that was. She didn't expect an answer but she got one.

"This is where all the city's metal comes from," said Victor, walking alongside her. "There's no naturally occurring metal here and even if there was we haven't got the means to process it. So when they need more they get it from the ship."

Iona was stunned by this. "But this mine's been disused for . . . I don't know how long it's been disused for."

"*Officially* it's disused. Stops people from coming down here. But they still send crews to get metal from time to time."

"Who's 'they'?"

"Oh, the supply department."

"And nobody ever asks where it comes from?"

Victor stopped and turned to Iona. "You'll find there's a lot of things nobody ever asks here. And you won't be able to understand how you never asked either."

"And they did all this . . . just to stop us from finding out there was a spaceship down here?"

Victor smiled. "No, there's more to it than that. But well done for remembering it's a spaceship. Took me a while to remember that."

"We both traveled on this, didn't we?"

"Yeah."

"Why was it called the—"

"*Mull of Kintyre*? I don't remember. Also I don't really remember you. Sorry."

"I don't either. I only remember tiny bits and pieces. Why did we forget?"

Victor looked somber suddenly. "Because we've lived too long. Ran out of space in our memories. Past a certain point it all gets vague."

"What do you mean, too long?"

Alyssa had gotten a long way ahead of them, but now she shouted through: "We can talk in the cargo hold. It's more comfortable there."

———

The cargo hold was mostly emptied out but it seemed to have some limited power—Alyssa turned on the lights and Iona could see three rows of citizens standing in the middle. They all faced the same way, arms by their sides, like troops waiting to be inspected. And Iona knew the reason for this before she saw it: the hatches on their backs had been left open. The only one whose hatch was not open—the nearest to her as she walked toward them—was Carter.

Iona turned and addressed Alyssa. "What are they?"

"You mean the citizens?"

"Yes."

"Highly advanced automata," said Victor.

"Made of . . . wood."

"Yep."

"By any sensible criteria they're intelligent—" started Alyssa, but Victor cut her off.

"Alyssa and I have had this debate *several* times."

"They have independent thought," Alyssa continued, "they have personalities. Iona—you teach them every day, *you* know they can learn."

"But they were made," said Iona.

"Yeah," said Victor. "Manufactured."

"Who made them?"

"Well, these days they make each other. At the Points of Origin."

Iona realized she'd never been assigned to design a Point of Origin, nor had she ever known what they were for—and as Victor had said, she'd never queried this.

"But who made the first one?" Iona said, referring to the citizens. She turned to Alyssa. "You?"

"What?" said Alyssa. "No. *They* did it." And she pointed to a two-seater sofa that had been placed against the wall.

At first Iona thought the sofa had two citizens sitting on it but as she walked closer she realized they were something different. They had a very similar shape to the citizens but were made of different materials—predominantly metal. They were old and corroded and parts of them were missing: both had exposed areas on their torsos, one was missing the lower part of its arm, the other had lost a leg. Wiring and circuitry could be seen through the holes. They had both clearly been inactive for a long time.

Like the ship itself, they were familiar.

"These were the service robots on the ship," said Victor, walking up behind her. "There were dozens of them once. Most of them were destroyed in the crash. The ones that were left started building replacements for themselves out of the materials they had on hand."

"To look after us after they were gone . . ." said Iona.

"It's incredible what they achieved. There's a small amount of metal inside each citizen—the brain and parts of the clockwork mechanism—but mostly it's wood. And as I say, they self-replicate."

Iona only half-listened to this. Something significant had been contained in what Victor just said but she hadn't immediately grasped it. She turned to him. "Crash?"

"Yeah," Victor began—and then stopped as he realized this was new information to her. He swallowed anxiously and turned to Alyssa.

Alyssa sighed and rolled her eyes at Victor. "I did tell you to let me do this. I was going to break it more gently."

"No, I remember," Iona said. "We're not from here. We came here to make a new home. But . . ."

There had been over four hundred people on board the ship. People traveling to a new life on a new planet.

The landing gear had failed. Iona had survived. Hardly anyone else had.

Iona sat on a chair Alyssa had found for her, struggling to process the knowledge that had come back into her mind. Victor had confirmed her recollections: his own memories were also very dim but chimed with what Iona managed to dredge up. Victor had then left her alone to process this, busying himself by looking inside Carter's hatch, tinkering with his insides. Even though she knew Carter was a machine now, Iona still found this unpleasant to look at.

"The citizens who 'die' don't actually *have* to be destroyed," said Victor. "Most of them are easy enough to repair. Often it's just that their brains get crudded up with all the data they've amassed, and you could correct that with a hard reset. But the city prefers to recycle the parts and make new ones—with each generation they refine the design, so—"

"They get better, faster," said Iona.

"The wooden parts burn in the furnace, the metal is retrieved for reuse."

"So you're saving them from the furnace because they're intelligent beings who deserve to live?"

"Nothing as altruistic as that, I'm afraid," said Alyssa as she brought over another chair and sat next to Iona.

"Did you come here on the ship too?"

"No, I only arrived a few weeks ago." This was why Alyssa had always seemed out of tune with the city. Iona had recognized this about her from the moment they met. But then Iona realized—

"Does that mean *you've* got a ship?"

Alyssa paused. "Yes, but—"

"Then you can get us home?"

"It's not functional. I don't know if it can be fixed. I've hidden it, but we have to get out of here first."

"Out of where?"

Alyssa and Victor exchanged glances. Victor broke off from his work and walked over to Iona.

"After we crashed," Victor began, "someone found us."

"What do you mean? Who?"

"They built this dome . . . but really it's a sort of cage, I suppose. They built it around us—and it goes right down into the ground, you can't dig under it—and they made the inside match our natural environment. Or *a* natural environment."

"The figures," said Iona. "You're talking about the figures. *They* put us in here."

"Yes."

"Why?"

"We don't know," said Alyssa, "but the dome preserves its subjects indefinitely. In here you don't age or die."

Iona blinked. "How long have we been here?"

Alyssa bit her tongue. "It's hard to tell exactly, because you traveled here through a wormhole and the time dilation effect isn't predictable—but our records suggest . . . well, it's at least seven hundred years."

Iona nodded, but it was too much to take in. She couldn't remember her childhood, her life on Earth, her family. She'd gained time by being in this dome—but she felt like she'd lost a great deal more. She felt like she'd lost herself.

"But . . . you only just got here?" Iona said. "From Earth?"

"Yes. They found me and realized I was like you, which I suppose is why they put me in here."

"But why did you come here? To find us?"

"No . . . not exactly, we assumed you'd all be dead by now. But—"

"The crash wasn't an accident, Iona," said Victor. He was holding out a sheaf of papers with words printed on them. "We had a stowaway."

———————

The deaths had started after they came out the other side of the wormhole.

The wormhole was an integral part of the journey, cutting out hundreds of light years. The technique had been tested and was believed to be entirely safe. Nobody was worried about it at all.

The initial deaths appeared to be heart failures, occurring in people who'd been thoroughly tested before the mission and found to be in good health. At first the ship's doctors theorized that traveling through the wormhole had weakened them somehow. They embarked on another series of tests, trying to find what had changed. They found small mutations in the bodies of the dead but didn't know what had caused them or how to stop them.

The mission continued and the deaths continued. The doctors kept carrying out tests: there was nothing else they could do.

One day they carried out some tests on a member of the crew and the results said he was not human. At this point the crew member in question started killing the doctors. The ship was put on high alert: the crew member had to be neutralized one way or another. Several more were killed but eventually the crew member was thrown from the airlock. They believed this was the end of it.

Or at least, most of them believed this. One of the surviving doctors kept studying the results of the tests they'd run on the bodies, as well as the tests on the crew member who'd turned out to be inhuman, and she developed a theory. She believed an intangible creature had come aboard the *Mull of Kintyre* while the ship was traveling through the wormhole. It had tried to inhabit the body of a crew member, but this process involved some physical mutation, which had killed the host. It had moved onto another crew member and killed that one too. This process had been repeated over and over until the creature managed to latch onto someone who didn't die, either because that person was physically different from the others or because the creature had learned from its earlier mistakes.

This doctor believed that if the creature could move from body to body, they couldn't be absolutely certain it wasn't still on board, hiding inside someone else. She insisted on running tests on every crew member but found nothing. The deaths stopped and the crew's worries subsided. They focused instead on reaching their destination.

Yet the doctor never stopped worrying about it. Maybe the creature was learning—maybe now it knew how to trick the tests and pass for human. She wrote all this down, not just in her report that was stored in the ship's systems but also on paper in case the systems failed. If she was right, it was too important to risk erasure. She didn't tell a lot of people about it because she worried any of them might be the creature—but she did tell her wife.

As Iona read the document she remembered Dr. Hanna Bradley. This memory wasn't vague and shapeless like the others that had drifted back to her—she saw Hanna's face and remembered the room they had shared on the *Mull of Kintyre* and how it had felt to be with her.

Iona looked up at Victor and Alyssa, who had stayed with her while she read the last thing her wife had written.

"She died in the crash, we think," Alyssa said, anticipating Iona's question. "If it's any consolation she was absolutely right. That report is an excellent piece of work."

It was no consolation at all.

"We reckon the thing wanted to strand us here so it sabotaged the ship," said Victor. "It wanted to cut us off from Earth."

"Possibly," said Alyssa. "Though it needs some of you alive, so if that was the plan it probably didn't intend to kill quite so many of you."

"How do you know so much about it?" asked Iona.

"This wasn't the only colony ship to be affected. Dozens of ships that went through those wormholes came out with unwanted passengers. Most of them lurked undetected on colonies—"

"What are they? What do they want?"

"We call them the Poramutantur, and all they do is fight each other. They've been at it for thousands of years. And they'll use anyone and anything as weapons. They inhabit the bodies of people with influence, they manipulate, they abuse trust—they set our colonies at war. Millions of people died. We've eliminated most of the Poramutantur now but it's taken centuries to undo the damage."

"It's our own fault," said Victor. "We went through the wormholes. We set them free."

"You were the *victims*. It's not your fault at all."

"So that's why you came," Iona said to Alyssa. "You think it's still here."

"I'm convinced it is. You *can't* kill them, we've tried. And if it was disguised as one of the crew it would've ended up in here with you."

"Alyssa's got a theory," said Victor, "that one of the dead citizens might know who the Poramutantur is because if one of them found out, the Poramutantur would destroy it to cover up. So we reactivate the dead, enter the program that makes them come down here, talk to them, ask them how they died, see if there's any clues there."

"I suppose you haven't found anything yet," said Iona,

"otherwise you'd—wait, *you* stole Weston's body, didn't you?"

"Yeah," said Victor sheepishly, "that was an experiment in sending a reprogrammed citizen to do the business. We usually do it covertly *before* the ceremony and replace the body with a dummy, but, er . . ." Victor gestured at a citizen whose body was singed and charred around the edges. "Our guy here didn't get a chance to do that so he tried to carry out his instructions via other means. He *just* managed to get out of the furnace with the body."

"It was a disaster," muttered Alyssa.

"To be fair I only had a few days' experience of fiddling with the programs."

"I know, which is exactly why I shouldn't have let you talk me into trying it."

Iona considered this. "You wanted to talk to Weston because you thought *I* was the Portamen . . . Porto-mut—"

"Poramutantur," corrected Alyssa.

"Thank you—you thought it was me, didn't you? And *you* came to me for tuition because—"

"Because I wanted to see if you gave yourself away, yes—look, don't be offended. I'm investigating *all* the human survivors of the crash. When I first met Victor I treated him as a suspect too."

"Isn't that a rather dangerous method of investigation

though? If I *was* this creature—"

"You'd have tried to kill me. But *I'd* have used *this*."
Alyssa produced from her coat pocket a tube that was
roughly the length and width of a wine bottle. Half the
tube was filled with electronic components, the other
with a sharp and chunky spike. It looked like the spike
shot out of the tube when activated. "This is to trap it
with when I find it. But I can't use it until I'm sure because, well, it would kill an ordinary human."

Iona felt tense as she looked at the spike and remembered how Alyssa had always had her hands in her pockets. "And you're sure it's *not* me now."

"Oh yes," said Alyssa cheerfully as she put the tube
back in her pocket. "So anyway, Weston's memories of his
death were all corrupted so to help him along—"

"You brought him to the newspaper offices."

"Yes, that went badly. When he realized he was supposed to be dead and therefore should have been cre-
mated, he very calmly sat down and finished the job. The
whole building went up with him."

"That's when we went to ground," Victor said. "We
worried the fire might be traced back to us."

"How did he start the fire?" asked Iona.

"You know when you rub two sticks together very
fast?" said Alyssa. "Well, that—but with his hands."

———————

The king's entourage surrounded him as he prepared to leave the tower—twenty-five of them standing two deep, giving him about two meters of clearance on all sides. These ones could be trusted, he told himself. They came into his chambers every day: they had ample opportunities to kill him if they wanted to, yet they never had. He felt sure they would protect him.

The king didn't make small talk or eye contact with his attendants. In recent days he had become very conscious of how he appeared to his subjects. He didn't want to offend or patronize them. Maybe they would interpret his silence as aloofness and grow to hate him for that reason. Maybe they all hated him already. Maybe the only reason they hadn't killed him was they felt too afraid.

The king stole a glance at the faces around him. They seemed dutifully impassive. He could read nothing in any of them.

The king sighed. "Come on, let's make a move."

The party stepped forward in unison and out of the front door.

The king emerged to find there was still a small crowd holding vigil outside the tower (didn't they have anything better to do?) and they responded to his appearance with astonishment. They followed him even when his attendants told them not to. And they were joined by others. The king heard shouts of encouragement and hollered felicitations. He hadn't come out here to seek their love or adulation. He just wanted to walk down the street.

———————

Iona emerged from the mouth of the mine shaft with Alyssa alongside her. From the old mining site it was only a short walk to the wall at the edge, and as Iona walked toward it she looked past the trees and up at what she'd always thought of as the sky. After all, it had a sun in it and clouds and sometimes it rained. But it struck her now there was no place where the wall ended and the sky began. The dome above their heads gave the illusion of day and night but it was not the sky.

"How big is this cage?" said Iona.

"That's a question that doesn't have a straightforward answer," said Alyssa, "because the inside is bigger than the outside."

Initially this didn't make sense to Iona—but then it did. "We're always expanding the city, and yet the wall is always the same distance from the city limits." There was about half a mile of woodland in between, and as far as she could remember, there always had been.

"The interior responds to your activity and expands to

give you all the space you need."

It took them about ten minutes of walking to reach the window. There were citizens standing there as usual and Alyssa wanted to keep out of earshot, so they hung back a little. To Iona the nature of the figures had always felt like an abstract question, a dinner party conversation about religion, forgotten the next day. It was not something that affected her day-to-day existence—or so she had always thought.

A figure appeared at the window and looked out impassively. Alyssa recalled her own theory that the window looked into a sort of parallel city and the figures were their counterparts. But now she saw this was quite, quite wrong. Embarrassingly so.

"Are they the native species here, then?" said Iona.

"Presumably," Alyssa replied. "I didn't get to talk to them before they caught me and put me in here."

"How did I not realize we were in a prison before now? I mean, I know we've forgotten all this stuff but—how can you see the walls every day and not remember—"

"The cage makes you think everything's normal. Stops you from questioning things. Stops you from trying to escape. You thought the citizens were real people because that was easier to believe than what was really happening to you, and the citizens acted like they were real people because they thought that was what you wanted."

"Then why's it stopped working?"

"Because I've disrupted things, perhaps? I'm sure it'll reassert itself in time. We all need to keep remembering what's real. Don't give it a chance to take over your mind again."

"But shouldn't we get out as quickly as—"

"We *will* get out *after* I've found what I'm looking for," said Alyssa impatiently. She turned back to the figures at the window. "Poor idiots. They've no idea what they've trapped in here. Or what it'll do to them if it gets out."

———

The king and his entourage had arrived at the Point of Return. He noted several officers from the Bureau of Order had been stationed by the door. The doors were closed. He walked up the steps and his entourage parted to let him through. The officers seemed very surprised to see him and they looked to each other for cues on what to do.

"What's this?" the king asked one of the officers, whose name badge read MILNER. She saluted him.

"We're stationed here until the man who attacked you has been put in the furnace," said Milner. "There's some concern that people might take their anger out on the body."

"Would it be a problem if they did?"

"Well, we're concerned that—"

"Doesn't matter—look, just let me in."

Milner looked uneasy. "We were told not to let anyone in—"

"Yeah, but I'm not anyone, I'm the *king*."

"—including you."

"What?"

"They said, 'Not even the king.'"

"That's outrageous. Who said that?"

The door opened and Saori emerged. "Your Highness. We thought you'd still be resting."

"I'm fine. Has she got this right? I'm not allowed in there?"

"Nobody is allowed in—"

"*I'm the king.*"

"The situation in here is delicate—"

"I know it is—*let me in*."

"Why?" said another voice: the voice of Clarence. He slipped through the gap between Saori's legs and peered up at the king.

"What are you doing here?" asked the king.

"I'm overseeing the disposal."

"Did *you* tell them not to let me in?"

"I only thought it would distress you—"

"What are you hiding from me?"

"Nothing. What are *you* doing here?"

"I'm going to do this myself. Feed him into the furnace myself. So I know he's really gone."

Clarence laughed.

"Don't laugh," said the king. "I didn't see him die. I want to know he's gone—I want to see him before he's burned and *I want to burn him.*"

"Don't you trust me to handle it?"

"I don't want you doing *everything* for me."

"You can't do it *all* on your own."

"Look, this is the only way I'll feel safe—I'm seeing, like, threats everywhere now and the only way I'll get back to how things were is if I—" The king became conscious that he should not have this argument in front of the bureau's employees. He looked up and addressed Saori. "I'm coming in and I'm doing this."

Saori nodded. "As you wish, Your Highness—but just wait here while I sweep the building for potential threats, please."

———

Iona and Alyssa had parted ways because Alyssa was going down to the city to collect another corpse, a citizen who had died under curious circumstances. After the Weston fiasco she thought it best to do it herself rather than send a citizen. Iona paused at the edge of the mine and looked back at the city, and a thought that had been nagging at her for a couple of hours now fully unfurled itself in her mind.

Iona had worked all her life as an architect and teacher of architecture. Her colleagues were architects or teachers or both. The people she taught went on to become architects, planners, and builders—those were the three subjects offered at the school and most students did a mix of them. Other people worked in the city's timber industry—planting trees, felling them, and sawing them up for building purposes. The mining industry, digging for stone, was smaller but still significant. There were also decorators and furniture crafters, the skills for which were learned on an apprenticeship basis.

Nearly everyone Iona knew fell under one of these categories. Further to this she could make a fair estimate of how many people were employed in making new buildings. All the other people she encountered in her daily life worked in government or service jobs, running the city—and having designed so many government buildings she had a good idea of how many people worked in them. She added all this up.

Whichever way she cut it, she had no idea what at least half the population of the city did. Did they just do nothing? What were they for?

More broadly, what was the *city* for? Did it just exist to grow bigger? Or was it for something else?

8

"**WHY DOES HE EVEN** *get* a ceremony?" the king said as he strode through the Point of Return, Clarence hurrying along at his feet, his entourage following at his back.

"Your Highness," said Clarence in a low voice, "I advise discretion—the gentleman's friends are waiting at the front."

"Ha!" said the king, pointing at his own head. "I've got a bruise right here that says there was *nothing* gentle about him."

"In answer to your question, the ceremony *will* be minimal, but we need people who knew him to act as witnesses. It's all procedure."

As they reached the front, one of Ward's friends stood and bowed to the king. "We're deeply sorry for the actions of—"

"I'm not interested," snapped the king without looking at her. Ward's friend dropped her head and looked away, as if worried the king might punch her on the way past. Before walking on any farther he turned to her and asked: "Why did he do it?" He said it calmly but pointedly.

"I . . . I don't . . ." She plainly didn't know but wanted to say something that was, somehow, useful.

"Did he ever talk about me?" said the king.

Ward's friends looked at each other. "Not in any unusual way," one of them said.

"What do you mean, unusual way?"

"Just that he talked about you like anyone else would."

"We can't understand it," another of the friends added. "He was just ordinary and quiet."

The king was about to ask more, but then one of the Point's undertakers, whose name was Bolton, approached him. "Can I help you, Your Highness?"

"Yes, you can," said the king.

———

The waiting room was through a door to the side of the stage. The king walked through it and found himself surrounded by bodies.

They lay on wheeled trolleys and shelves, stacked three high. He was well aware of how many people died in the city every day, thanks to the list that came in each letter. But seeing it expressed in words was quite different from seeing it expressed in racks of dead bodies waiting to be burned. Once upon a time they'd been useful citizens and now they weren't, so the city was going to burn them and put the energy back into itself—the last useful thing they could do.

Everyone was replaced eventually—except the king. At least he assumed that was the case. He'd never asked. He didn't want to ask. Just in case it had never occurred to anyone that he *could* be replaced.

The waiting room was not wide and the king had to strip his entourage down to four, otherwise it would have been terribly crowded in there. Clarence trotted in with them.

"Which of these is him?" the king asked Bolton.

Bolton stepped over to a body and indicated it with an open palm. The king joined her at the side of the trolley.

"Is this Ward, then?"

Bolton nodded.

The king looked the body up and down. He *did* look ordinary. He could be anyone.

Clarence leaped up and sat just next to the dead citizen's head. He craned his neck, moved his face closer to the body, and sniffed the skin in several places.

The king grimaced. "What the—Clarence, that's disgusting."

Clarence looked up at the king and Bolton. "This isn't Ward."

"What?" said the king. "How do you know?"

"I was there when he was caught, I remember his smell."

"But it must—" began Bolton, then stopped. "Oh my god. It isn't him."

"Then who the hell is it?" said the king.

"I don't know," said Clarence.

"But you know *everyone*."

"That's the most troubling thing."

"Where *is* he then?"

———————

"Can you look at what else is in their heads?" said Iona as she walked back into the cargo bay.

Victor was busy toying with the switches inside one of his cohort of citizens. He looked up. "Like what?"

Iona was about to speak when she realized the citizen he was working on was Carter. She looked into Carter's "eyes" and the illusion of a human face flitted across her vision. She tried to hold the face in her mind, see her colleague as she used to, but then she remembered his face was all part of the illusion that had kept her trapped here. If she saw it again that would be a bad sign.

Victor gestured at Carter. "Is there something you want to get out of him?"

Iona shook her head. "Not him specifically—in fact one of the others would be better." She hoped this theory would stand up when she said it aloud. "Right, by my reckoning at least half the people in this city don't do anything. They don't have jobs, or at least not that I know of, and I've designed nearly every type of office and factory we've got."

Victor paused a moment while he took this in. "Okay, that's true."

"Why is that?"

"Makes the city look more . . . like a city if it's got more people in it, I guess."

"Maybe—but . . . they were made to serve us. We've been lulled into believing they're just people like us, and they've gone along with that because they thought it was what we wanted. But think about it—if they *were* built to serve us, what would they be doing?"

"Looking after us."

"And if they know we're locked in a cage, the best way to look after us would be . . ."

Victor didn't take long to arrive at an answer: "To get us out."

"And you've seen them sitting at home, right? Just sat there facing each other. What if *all* of them, the ones who aren't doing jobs, are working on *exactly* that problem?"

Victor tapped a screwdriver against the palm of his hand, then he reached into Carter's hatch. "Let's find out."

"What kind of an operation is this?" shouted the king when it became apparent that Ward's body had entirely vanished from the waiting room.

"It must have been stolen," Bolton said.

"Who's stealing *bodies*? I want him found—*now*!"

The king's attendants scattered in search of Ward's corpse. So did everyone who worked at the Point. This meant Clarence and the king were suddenly alone.

"Calm down, Your Highness," said Clarence, which annoyed the king.

"Why's everything going wrong all of a sudden? *Everything's* going wrong."

"It must all be connected. It can't be a coincidence."

"Why not?"

"Because it's all happening at the same time."

"But that's what a coincidence is, isn't it? It's things happening at the same time."

"Trust me, Your Highness. When we find the connection we'll be able to solve *all* these problems."

The king grunted, then returned his attention to the body on the trolley that was not Ward. "What's wrong with his face?"

"He's dead."

"Apart from that. There's just something . . . off about him." The king grew increasingly agitated.

"Lie down," said Clarence.

"What?"

"Lie down."

"On the floor? It's all dirty."

"Use one of the spare trolleys."

"But they've had dead people on them."

"They clean them afterward."

"I can't do this in the middle of a public building."

"Who's going to see? They're all busy looking for Ward."

The king sighed, clambered onto a spare trolley, and lay facedown. Clarence hopped from trolley to trolley, making his way to the king's side. With claws carefully retracted, Clarence stepped up onto the king's back and kneaded his shoulders with his paws.

"Ohh that's good," said the king.

"I knew that was what you needed."

"I'm finding this all really stressful."

"Understandably."

"I just wish I understood why it was all—Wait, go back. There's a knot just there."

Clarence shifted his paw. "There?"

"No. You had it a second ago. Bottom of the shoulder blade. That's it. Aaaah. Ow!"

"Sorry, does that hurt?"

"Yeah, but in a good way. What do you think they're up to?"

"Who?"

"Whoever's doing all this."

"I can't imagine."

"I mean what are they trying to *achieve*?"

Clarence didn't answer. He just kept kneading.

The king was silent for a few moments, then said: "Do you think there are too many people?"

Clarence stopped kneading. "Why do you say that?"

"I'm just trying to think of what's changed, what might have made people unhappy so they attack me and burn stuff down. The main thing is there are more people now and the city's bigger. Maybe the bigger the city gets, the . . . smaller people feel."

"What utter nonsense."

"No need to bite my head off."

Clarence paused. "We can't let the city stagnate. It has to grow."

"But how can you know—"

The conversation ended because the door opened and Saori walked in, flanked by her operatives. She saw the king lying on a trolley with Clarence perched on his back and she clearly felt she'd interrupted something she shouldn't have.

"Don't you knock?" asked the king, cementing this impression. He rose, forcing Clarence to leap awkwardly to the floor.

"I'm sorry, Your Highness," said Saori. "I just wanted to tell you we've found Ward."

"*Yes!*" said the king, punching the air.

"Excellent!" said Clarence, grinning.

"But there's something else," Saori added. "He's not dead."

The king and Clarence looked at each other. The king laughed, because surely this must be a joke. Clarence didn't laugh.

"His body wasn't stolen," said Saori. "He's alive and someone helped him escape."

As afternoon gave way to evening, Iona helped Victor to probe the artificial brains of the citizens. She even felt like she was starting to understand how they worked. She and Victor had isolated the ones with no known job, reactivated them, and asked them questions. The question of what they actually did elicited a blank response, as if they simply didn't comprehend it. They reacted as though there was no reason to think they would do anything.

Iona wondered if this was a side effect of them having died, but a test with some of the others revealed they all remembered their lives in the city well enough. The ones who apparently did nothing were either genuinely doing nothing or they were doing something they weren't talking about.

Victor had managed to work out some of the citizens' programming language, which was input via the numbered switches in the cavity; it was he who had come up with the sequence that was written on the instructions Iona had found. He entered commands and each citizen would speak reams of code that Iona wrote down as quickly as she could. Victor analyzed this code and tried to locate the citizens' security protocols. There were several failures along the way—in resetting one citizen they wiped its entire memory. But eventually they established there was a code-phrase—"starlit sky"—that released the information they were looking for.

Now the citizens told a different story. They explained how they got together in pairs—different pairs each day, so they heard different points of view. Together they analyzed the composition of the dome walls and discussed available implements to break through it. They talked about the environmental controls for the dome and how they might possibly be accessed from the inside. They pondered the exact location of the door, what the mechanics of it might be, what lock it might use and how it might be picked. They theorized, based on their limited observations, on the nature of their captors, how their language worked, and how they might be induced to open the door. Every citizen was aware of the many attempts that had been made in the past and this ensured they did not replicate work that had previously been done. The best idea they had come up with so far was that the interior of the dome could not continue to expand indefinitely, and if they continued to build a larger and larger humanesque settlement, eventually it would stretch to breaking point and an opportunity to escape might present itself. But this was just a theory so far.

In short, Iona was right. The citizens had been trying to find a way out of this cage for centuries. The length of time this had been happening, and the volume of processing power dedicated to it, led Iona to wonder if perhaps there *was* no way out. Surely if there was they'd have worked it out by now.

But more curiously, they had kept these efforts from the humans all this time. Neither Iona nor Victor could see why the citizens would do this. Victor felt certain someone had interfered with their programming and introduced this code-phrase, "starlit sky," as a security measure to block the humans' access to the citizens' true work.

So caught up were Iona and Victor with this discovery that it was quite late before they started to worry that Alyssa wasn't back yet. Victor went out into the city to look for her. Iona stayed here in case Alyssa came back while he was gone.

Iona now felt confident in her operation of the citizens and continued to question them about their attempts to break out of the cage. A new and promising line of research had opened up, involving the lock on the door.

"Where is the door?" Iona asked one of the citizens.

Next to the window, the citizen told her. The citizens who kept watch on the window had seen it open when the new human had been deposited inside. Then the door had vanished again, invisible and impossible to locate.

Iona realized this "new human" was Alyssa. Her entry into the dome had given the citizens a vital insight into how the door, and its lock, functioned. With this knowledge they believed it was possible to fashion a device that would trigger the lock from the inside. A citizen was explaining to Iona what form they believed this might take when Victor returned, clutching a hastily printed late edition of the newspaper. "She got caught," he said.

"What?"

"Did you hear about the king getting attacked?"

"By Alyssa?"

"No, just by some random bloke on the street. There was a crowd there to see the king and they beat the guy to death."

"Bloody hell."

"Alyssa was breaking in to steal his body in case there

was a lead—"

"In case the Poramutantur is the king?"

"Exactly. But they caught her, so she's being charged with helping a criminal escape, and she'd reactivated him so there's questions being asked because everyone thought he was dead . . ." He threw the newspaper to the floor. "Shit."

"What do we do?"

Victor looked around, shaking his head. "We can't do any of this without Alyssa. She's the only one who knows how to trap this creature. We've got to break her out."

9

THE KING TOOK A seat opposite Ward. He'd been waiting for this for several hours.

The king couldn't remember the last time he'd spent so much time outside the tower. The bureau staff had told him they needed to question Ward first, try to find out how he'd fooled everyone into thinking he was dead, ask him who the woman was who'd helped him escape. This was all important procedure and the king was willing to be patient.

The king had filled the time by personally thanking the citizens who had caught Ward and his accomplice and telling their superiors they should be given an official commendation. On discovering the bureau had no system of commendations he had invented one and ordered some special badges to be designed. He'd then had some dinner sent over, which he had eaten alone in an unoccupied office, and after that held discussions with bureau staff about how they could crack down on this sort of extremism and improve security for law-abiding citizens.

Eventually, at long last, he'd been told he could speak to Ward.

Ward was in restraints because he'd tried to escape. It occurred to the king that he could just go over there and give Ward a kicking. He doubted anyone would stop him or protest. But the king hadn't come here for revenge, he'd come for a confrontation. In this sense it was lucky that Ward had come back from seemingly being dead, although the king was puzzled and disturbed that this had come to pass.

Ward stared back at the king. He hadn't reacted to the king's entrance at all. You'd think coming face-to-face with the man you clubbed down in the street would provoke some reaction—fear, hate, contrition, satisfaction maybe? He'd shown nothing.

"You're probably wondering why I'm here," said the king.

Ward didn't speak.

"I just want to know why you did it," the king went on. "Was it personal? Do you hate me? Did you want to hurt me? Kill me? Or were you just trying to make a point?"

Still no reaction.

"I don't care if you tell me or not. I just wanted to ask, you know. If you had a point, I thought . . ." The king was finding it hard to keep on track while getting no reaction. "Because you know, if there was no point, why *do* it?"

The citizen stared straight ahead. Possibly at the king, possibly past him.

The king tapped his foot, then leaned forward. "Did I do something to you? How can I have? I never do anything." A new thought occurred. "Is it something I *didn't* do? That's it, isn't it?"

The king stood up, paced around a bit, and then kicked the leg of the table, causing the table to jump.

Ward didn't flinch.

"Tell me!" said the king, gripping the back of his chair. Ward might as well have stayed dead for all the good this was doing. The king felt like flinging the chair across the room—

But then he stopped. This guy was nothing. Literally nothing. The king resolved not to let him affect his decisions or actions or mood in any way.

"Fine," the king said, striding back toward the door. "If you've nothing to say, I'll tell them they can burn you."

As he left the room he glanced back, looking in vain for any sign he'd reached Ward at all.

———

Victor had drawn up a set of plans for Iona to use, pointing out it was no different from what she'd done to Carter, it just involved putting the switches into different positions. This may have been true but it didn't mean she felt any more at ease with reprogramming beings who, until this morning, she had regarded as people just like herself. She had no time to indulge such qualms, however.

"What exactly will this make them do?" Iona asked while they each worked their way along a line of citizens, reaching into the cavities in their backs and entering Victor's new program, which he had kept as simple as possible. Iona would have liked it to be simpler—she could follow it okay but inputting it was tedious and moving the tiny switches hurt her fingers.

"It *should* make them storm the bureau," said Victor.

"I hope it's rather more . . . *precise* than your effort at getting Weston out."

"I did *get* him out, didn't I?" muttered Victor. "Anyway we need to move quickly—the guy who attacked the king is lined up to be burned alive and Alyssa might be next."

"But he was a citizen, wasn't he?"

"So?"

"So Alyssa's not . . . I mean they wouldn't burn a *real* person alive, would they?"

"You're assuming this decision's being made by someone who knows the difference."

With this sobering thought in mind Iona moved onto

her third citizen. Victor was working much faster and was already finishing his fifth.

"How did you learn how to do this?" Iona asked him.

"Lots of trial and error. And also . . . I think this used to be my job, back on the ship. It feels familiar. Do you remember what you were?"

"Oh, I think I was always an architect. I think I was meant to build the colony when we got here." She knew she was good at what she did. She felt like a person who had trained and honed her skills. She felt like someone they *would* send to build a city on a new world. She'd been so modest about her ability all these years and now she felt like that modesty had been taken advantage of.

Iona kept on entering the program. Whatever job she'd done back on the ship, she was sure it wasn't this.

———

The king barged into Saori Kagawa's office and interrupted her while she was talking to a colleague (nobody he knew and therefore nobody important). "Where's Clarence?" he said.

"He's talking to the woman who helped Ward escape," Saori replied after the colleague had made her excuses and left.

"Why's he doing that?"

"We need to know more about her. She may have other associates."

"Okay, that makes sense but why's Clarence the one talking to her?"

"He wanted to."

The king leaned over the desk. "You don't take orders from Clarence."

Saori stared back at him, calm. He could never quite assert himself with her and he wasn't sure why. He was never sure if she liked him or not and for some reason it mattered to him. He didn't get that vibe from anyone else in the city.

"I know I don't," she replied.

"Good."

"He didn't order me. It was a request and I decided to grant it. Should I have run it by you first?"

"No," said the king, straightening up. "I'm just making sure you know what's what." He walked out.

———

Clarence was sitting on the table in the interview room, which brought him up to eye level with Alyssa. She slumped in the chair opposite, glowering back at him from behind curtains of long curly hair. As the king walked into the room he caught the end of her sentence—she was saying, "There's just me. Nobody else"—then she broke off. Both Clarence and Alyssa turned to look at the king.

Briefly the king saw an eager light in the young woman's eyes. He was worried she might try to kill him. But then he realized her hands were tied behind her back.

Clarence hopped off the table, trotted toward the king, and said, "What are you doing in here?"

"Are you—?" Alyssa began, but Clarence cut her off.

"Shut up," Clarence said without looking back at her. "I must speak to you outside, Your Highness." He ushered the king back through the door and told him to close it.

"What's up with you?" said the king.

"She's a very dangerous woman who wants you *dead*," said Clarence.

"What?"

"*She* planned the attack on you—Ward was just a stooge. You shouldn't go anywhere near her."

"But . . . she's got no weapons and her hands are tied behind her back—"

"It's not worth the risk—*stay away*."

"Okay." The king felt shaken: he'd just convinced himself the attack was nothing to worry about. "But why?"

"She's set up a network of agents to plot the overthrow of your rule. She's confessed to everything. *She* burned down the newspaper offices."

"Bloody hell," said the king. He felt even angrier about that than the assault.

"She's given us other names but it's clear there are people she's still protecting—I told you this wasn't a coincidence."

The king consciously steadied his breathing. "What are we going to do?"

"Strong action now can stop this in its tracks. The statute books do specify the sentence for treason—it hasn't been used in a very long time, but this seems a clear-cut case . . ."

"Alright, what is it?"

Clarence turned and nodded to a member of the bureau staff who stood unobtrusively nearby holding a book of law. Most of the city's laws related to planning and safety and evidently this volume, which dealt with acts of violence and sedition, had rarely been consulted—the edges of its pages were clean. The staffer opened the book, walked over to the king, and indicated a regulation.

The king peered over and read it. His eyebrows shot up. "That's brutal."

"It is what the law says—in fact *you* made this law."

"Really? I don't remember that at all."

"It *was* quite some time ago."

This sort of thing wasn't unknown—the king made a lot of offhand comments in the heat of anger or annoyance, and his attendants did sometimes take them as policy and have them enshrined in law. "Okay then," he said. "I guess we need to make an example of her."

"Exactly—and we should make it an open event so anyone can come."

The king nodded. "And I should be there too."

"I don't think that's necessary—"

"No, it *is* necessary because I want to show people I'm not afraid and also, if I'm there more people will come."

"I still think—"

"Yeah, great, you keep thinking, but tell everyone I'll be there. When's this happening?"

"Tomorrow morning."

"As soon as that?"

"Yes, so you should get some sleep. You must be tired. Go back to the tower."

The king nodded. "Fair enough."

Clarence nodded at the cell door. "Could you open that for me, please?"

The king did so and as Clarence trotted back inside the room the king caught another glimpse of the villain seated at the table. She grimaced at Clarence, then turned a look on the king, which puzzled him. She didn't look at him with hatred or contempt, but . . . concern?

Then the door swung closed.

———————

It was deep into downtime when they emerged from the mouth of the old mine. Victor walked at the front, Iona at the rear. Between them walked thirty-eight citizens. Iona caught a glimpse of the city as they crested the hill: it all looked quiet.

Just before they reached the edge of the suburbs, the citizens started to peel off and head down different streets. This was part of their programming: they would take different routes to the bureau to avoid attracting attention. Before long Iona and Victor were walking with just two other citizens following closely behind. This small group would not seem unduly suspicious.

Some part of Iona, in the face of everything, still nurtured some notion of going back to her old life, of just quietly going home and leaving Victor and Alyssa to it. She couldn't help but think of her house and the school as "normal." Things were simpler before she knew the truth, before she'd remembered what she'd lost. But as they passed other citizens going about their business—rickshaw drivers, night-shift construction workers—the impossibility of this became clear. She saw the citizens differently now and she didn't want to go back to the school, see her old colleagues, her friends. She would know what they were really made of, she would detect the artificial patterns in their responses. She saw through the thinness of her old life. She couldn't go back and pretend—and if others had any clue about what she'd done today, they wouldn't regard her as normal either.

She tried to think about what her life would be like after this.

Then they reached the bureau, and there were other things to think about.

———

The other reprogrammed citizens had all concealed themselves in the streets near the bureau, waiting for Victor's signal. Iona couldn't see them but Victor was confident they'd be there. Iona fretted she'd made a mistake in replicating Victor's program: a single misplaced digit might have sent a citizen somewhere else entirely.

Victor had brought Alyssa's electric torch with him from the ship and this was the agreed signal for the attack to begin. They'd also brought some sharp-edged tools that were actually designed for hacking vegetation away from overgrown areas when setting up camp, but they had potential as weapons, were retractable, and could be concealed under clothing, and most importantly they didn't require any power source.

"You don't have to come inside," Victor told Iona. "It might be just as useful to have someone waiting out here to help Alyssa get away—"

"I'm coming inside," Iona replied, rather irritated by the implication she was too old and incapable of helping.

Victor nodded, turned on the torch, and shone it around the nearby buildings, spreading its light. There was no mistaking it—all forms of light native to the city looked completely different from this.

The movement began at once: the citizens who'd been watching for the signal emerged from hiding and rushed toward the bureau. Iona and Victor rushed with them and suddenly it all felt real and it hit home that she might actually die here. *Could* she die here? The dome was supposedly keeping them all alive, but did it only stop them from aging or developing diseases? Could it reckon with a fatal wound as well?

The bureau was better guarded than usual but it was still unprepared for a massed attack. Though the reprogrammed citizens were untrained they attacked with complete abandon, unconcerned for their personal safety. Iona and Victor walked at the back, letting their citizen army go first. The guards at the door had been dealt with swiftly and Iona passed their broken bodies on the way inside. She didn't look at them too long, telling herself they were only wood.

Iona's intimate knowledge of the layout of the bureau was invaluable. The citizens had been programmed with clear instructions on where to go and what to do when they got there. The rescue party started heading up the stairs. Thanks to the element of surprise, thus far they had sustained only minor injuries.

As they climbed to the higher levels Iona could hear guards from the detention level coming down to confront them. There were more clashes; some of their party fell. Iona reached the detention level and for the first time she had to use her weapon as a guard rushed at her. She lashed out as hard as she could, barely aiming at all. As the weapon made contact it jarred her shoulder and stung her hands but it worked. The guard's head came clean off.

Iona turned her eyes away and kept running.

She checked the first cell she came to but it was empty. So was the second. Victor was not far behind, along with some of their citizens—all of them swarmed around the detention level searching for Alyssa.

Alyssa wasn't there.

"Is there anywhere else she could be?" demanded Victor. He and Iona stood in one of the cells, looking around as if there was anywhere a person could hide in here.

Outside their citizens were still searching—but reinforcements were arriving to protect the bureau and clashes were beginning again in the corridor.

"I don't know," said Iona. "The newspaper said she was in custody. This is custody, so—"

The door of the cell closed behind them and the bolt was swung into place.

10

EVERY SEAT AT THE Point of Return was occupied despite the early hour, and despite the event only having been announced at dawn. The aisles were packed with standing spectators and the doorway thronged with latecomers jostling for a view. All of them had been told that if they came they would see something special. Few of them, however, believed the rumor that the king would appear here personally. Surely not after the recent attack on him—he'd never risk it.

This meant that when the king, flanked by four guards, entered through the front door and walked down the aisle a gratifying ripple of excitement spread through the crowd. He glanced to where Clarence sat atop one of the decorative carved scrolls that adorned the wall to the right of the stage.

Clarence nodded.

The king let the hubbub go on for a few seconds, then raised a hand and everyone fell silent.

Good.

The king said nothing. Instead he signaled to the doorway that led through to the waiting room and two trolleys were brought out by attendants. They were just like the trolleys used every day here at the Point, with one important modification—thick restraints had been fitted to each one, holding the subject by the wrists and ankles. These restraints were not usually necessary because the occupants of the trolleys were usually dead.

One of the trolleys held Ward, the other held Alyssa.

Alyssa maintained an impassive countenance in the face of the audience's hushed scrutiny as the trolleys reached the center of the stage—a space the king had now vacated, stepping to one side—and were tilted so Alyssa and Ward were almost upright. Now they had no choice but to face the people.

The king pointed to the people on the trolleys and addressed the audience.

"*He* is the man who attacked me. But *she* ordered the attack. And *she* started the fire."

For a moment the crowd considered what the king had said. The king took this opportunity to move farther out of the way.

Then the bombardment began.

Everyone, it seemed, in the first dozen rows had come prepared: all had brought bits of old furniture or discarded building materials and they flung it at the criminals. Ward remained entirely passive, just as he'd been since his arrest, and Alyssa did her best to follow suit. She bit her lip, managed not to cry out in pain, and waited for the crowd to run out of ammunition—which, after less than a minute, they did. However, they then started to pull pieces off the seats so they could throw those, and the king's guards were forced to intervene.

Their rage was a bit disturbing. But at least they cared.

The king held up a hand and walked back to the center of the stage. The crowd fell silent again.

The king turned and gestured to the attendants. This time the furnace doors opened, revealing the inferno within. A wild cheer came from the crowd. Alyssa was unable to see the fire but she could feel its heat. From a distance people might infer from her apparent lack of reaction that death somehow did not matter to her. But the king was close enough, and perceptive enough, to see on her face genuine dread and despair.

The trolleys were unceremoniously dropped back into their previous position and the attendants started to wheel Ward toward the furnace. In moments they would do the same to Alyssa. She turned her head to face the king and spoke to him—loud enough for him to hear but not loud enough for the unruly crowd, who were chattering with anticipation at the punishment to come.

She said: "Steve."

The king was astonished. He turned and stared at

Alyssa and felt panic rising within himself. He wanted to walk away from her, down the aisle and out of the building—but at the same time he wanted to know how Alyssa knew that was his name when he had all but forgotten it himself.

Behind them Ward was being fed into the furnace. The king had been especially looking forward to that part but now that it was happening he didn't even turn to look.

"Steve—you came here on a ship, the *Mull of Kintyre*," Alyssa went on. "This city is a cage and there's something trapped in here with you; I thought perhaps it *was* you but now I know it's not—"

But it was Alyssa's turn for the furnace. The attendants started to wheel her away and her voice was lost in the baying of the crowd. The king held up a hand, trying to stop them, but the attendants were facing away and couldn't hear him. She was pushed toward the flames, the mob screaming for her to be destroyed, and all the king could do was stand and watch. He wanted more time to think, he felt like telling everyone to stop for a moment—but for all his power and influence, he lacked the courage to intervene.

As Alyssa vanished into the furnace, the king saw the heat singe her hair but she closed her eyes and remained silent. Her resolve held until the furnace doors shut behind her, but then she let out screams that penetrated the doors and rang out through the hall. At first this brought cathartic enjoyment to the crowd but as it went on, discomfort and unease set in.

The king felt wretched.

Something touched the king's ankles and he started in surprise. It was Clarence, brushing around his legs. A deep purr came from his throat.

———

"Good news, Your Highness," were the words that greeted the king as he stepped through the side door of the memorial parlor and into the waiting room. They were spoken by Saori Kagawa, who was waiting for him there.

"Right," muttered the king, swiftly closing the door before Clarence could follow. He didn't want to talk to anyone. Alyssa's screams had cut through him in a way he hadn't expected and he really, really wished he'd spoken out and stopped it from happening. He stared down at the floor.

"You were told of the attack on the bureau last night?" said Saori.

"Yeah . . ." His attendants had told him about it while he was getting dressed this morning.

"We've questioned the perpetrators. They came to liberate Alyssa, not realizing we'd already moved her here. So we've captured more of her network."

The king didn't look up. Saori seemed puzzled by his lack of reaction but didn't say anything.

"Yeah," the king said finally. "Good." He was far from sure that this was the real problem, or if it was a problem at all. What Alyssa had said to him just before she died was true. There was a spaceship called the *Mull of Kintyre* and his name was Steve.

"Two of them are quite high-ranking citizens," Saori went on, trying to prompt more of a response. "An architect and teacher called Iona Taylor, and a policymaker in the planning department called Victor Musa."

The king looked up. "I know those names."

"You might have met them."

"I think I have."

"In the course of business."

"Maybe." But the king knew the names were familiar for other reasons.

The king walked past Saori, toward the door. "Well done," he said over his shoulder.

"What do you want done with them?"

"Nothing." He was almost through the doorway now.

"What do you mean, nothing?"

"I mean *nothing*," snapped the king, turning back to her. "Just keep them where they are and . . ." He waved an arm. "Await my instructions, alright? And no I don't know *when* I'll have instructions so just *wait*—"

The king stopped talking. For several moments he just stared at Saori as though seeing her for the first time. Then he said in a quiet voice: "Were *you* on the ship?" They were alone in the room but he was worried someone—he didn't know who, but *someone*—might be listening.

"What ship?" said Saori. It wasn't a word anyone in the city ever used. The king didn't know where he'd learned it. But as Saori repeated it back to him the king noticed she hadn't asked, *What is a ship?* She'd simply asked, *What ship?*

"The spaceship," the king replied, modifying the rootless word to produce another one. "It was called the *Mull of Kintyre*. Were you on it?"

Saori didn't reply. The king took her frozen expression for incomprehension.

"Never mind," he said and stormed out of the Point, hoping Saori wouldn't tell anyone he'd gone weird on her.

———

Iona had not been allowed to sleep before being removed from the cell she and Victor had been shut in. They'd put her in another room and questioned her. Standard tactic, get people when they were tired and they let things slip they otherwise wouldn't. It didn't matter anyway—their citizen army answered every question they were asked truthfully, as Victor hadn't been able to include anything as sophisticated as deception in his program. So their entire plan had been laid bare.

Now Iona had been placed in a new cell and though she was allowed to sleep she couldn't, despite exhaustion. Anxiety gnawed at her—fears about what had happened to Alyssa, about what would happen to her and Victor, about whether the Poramutantur would now get out. She wondered how close the citizens were to cracking the lock.

As Iona pondered this question her eyes went to the door of her cell. Through the small grille window in the center she could see the back of a citizen's head. It had been posted to stand guard. This meant long, long hours of doing basically nothing: standing and staring straight ahead.

This seemed a considerable waste of processing power. Surely the sensible thing to do was to put the guards to work on the problem of escaping the cage.

Maybe whoever had set this thing in motion *was* sensible.

Iona walked to the door, put her mouth close to the

grille, and quietly said, "Starlit sky."

The guard told her it was in the midst of processing data and asked if she would like a progress report.

Iona said she would like this very much.

———————

The king sat by his window and stared out across the city. He had told everyone he was not to be disturbed but as usual Clarence assumed this didn't include him. The cat paced in and out of the chambers and sometimes the king could hear him talking to someone outside. The bureau was still searching for more of Alyssa's associates. Clarence seemed to believe this was why the king was looking out of the window, that he was thinking about where traitors might still be lurking. But he wasn't thinking about that at all.

Clarence hopped up to the windowsill and shared the king's view.

After they'd both been sitting there a while in silence, the king said: "Maybe it's time to let someone else have a go."

"A go at what?"

"Being king."

"Don't be ridiculous."

"Why's that ridiculous?"

"Who else could do the job?"

"Anyone. What do I even do? Why do we even have a king? Everything runs itself."

"That's not true."

"Well yeah, *you* run most of it."

"No no no. I just advise."

"You could advise someone else, doesn't have to be me."

"What would you do?"

"Lots of things. I'd like to get into research."

"Research?"

"Yeah, just . . . finding out how things work. We're always making the city bigger and bigger and it seems like we never stop to think about, like, things *outside* the city—"

Clarence was staring at the king like he'd brought up a distasteful subject.

"It was just an idea." The king took off his crown, turned it over in his hands. "But I did wonder, though—who would I be if I wasn't the king?"

"Well, this is what I'm saying—you'd have nothing to do."

"I don't mean what would I *do*. Everyone calls me the king. If I wasn't king, what would my name be?"

"I don't know."

"You know *everything*," said the king insistently. "Why

haven't I got a name, Clarence?"

"You don't need a name."

"Everyone else has got a name."

"Then we'll get you one, if it makes you feel better."

The king went back to looking out of the window. He knew he had a name. He just wanted to see if Clarence knew it.

For the first time Iona was taking part in the kind of discussion the citizens had been engaging in for years, but which she had always felt excluded from. Without turning around the guard spoke to her in a calm, measured voice, explaining the latest thinking on how the door used by the figures could be opened. The citizens had built a virtual model of the door in their minds and all of them now shared it. The guard described the theoretical opening device they were designing. Iona, who knew a thing or two about doors and locks, responded with ideas of her own.

The only frustrating part for Iona was that she couldn't tell the citizen to open her cell. She could ask it for information and she could feed it information, but she couldn't give it commands. It ought to obey her—that was why it had been made in the first place—but someone had gotten inside its programming and locked her out.

Down the years, citizen had talked to citizen about the problem of the door but they had never spoken to the humans about it: they had just gotten on with the job. The guard now had access to a whole new perspective. It was the cognitive equivalent of a sprint for the finish line.

Iona wasn't sure just how close they were to finishing when she heard footsteps approaching from down the corridor. She stepped away from the door. The guard had fallen silent and from outward appearances it seemed just to be guarding. A voice told it to move aside and it did so. Then the door to the cell opened and Saori Kagawa stepped inside.

Saori had not been involved in Iona's interrogation. A great deal had changed since Iona last saw her at the site of the fire. The true nature of the citizens had since been revealed to Iona and now she could see Saori was not one of them. She was human. Everyone else she'd spoken to at the bureau had been a citizen.

But why was Saori here in person? Was there something else she needed to know? They'd told the bureau staff everything. They'd even explained the nature of the cage, but to no response—as if the citizens weren't supposed to acknowledge this fact, not in the presence of humans.

Saori didn't take a seat. She looked Iona up and down.

If Saori was a human then presumably she came here on the ship. Which meant it was also possible she was the Poramutantur. The situation required caution.

"Can I help you?" Iona asked.

"How long had you known Alyssa for?"

"Only a few days."

"Because there's no record of her, you see. We have records of everyone in the city but not her. Did you steal her record? Destroy it? Or did she?"

"No. Alyssa comes from—"

"She's dead," said Saori and Iona could hear something unsteady in her voice. "We burned her. She was plotting to kill the king."

"That's not true," Iona replied. She could see Saori was confused. Hopefully this was a sign she was starting to work her way through the fog that had been thrown around her perceptions.

"We've got evidence. She confessed."

"Confessed? Who to?"

"Clarence."

"Who's Clarence?"

"The king's . . . the king's cat, of course." As she spoke a change came over Saori's expression, as if she had suddenly realized the absurdity of what she'd just said.

Clarence had not spent all these years in the company of the king without learning how to sense his mood. Things were changing. The intrusion of Alyssa had disrupted the city, possibly fatally—but it might also release him before everything collapsed.

King's Tower had many spare rooms below the king's chambers. The king never went in any of them. Clarence opened the door to one of them now. Inside the room was a table and two chairs, where two citizens sat opposite one another.

Clarence hopped up on the table, faced one of the citizens, and said: "Starlit sky."

Iona knew the king had a cat—he sometimes mentioned this fact in his columns—but she didn't know anything else about it. It was the only cat in the city—another of those privileges that were exclusive to the king. However, Iona had never heard anything about the cat acting as an advisor to the king, which Saori had just claimed as if it was perfectly normal.

Saori explained that Clarence's position, and his proximity to the king, gave him the ability to assume authority in such situations—and the simple fact was that when he did get involved in situations they were always resolved. It didn't happen often but it was a natural part of how the city worked.

Yet he was a cat. This executive power was routinely handed to a cat.

"But everything Clarence does is on the king's behalf," Saori stated. "It's all sanctioned. It's safer for Clarence to handle it so the king doesn't have to leave the tower—I mean we all saw what happened last time he left the tower."

"But the king doesn't get citizens to do this stuff," said Iona. "He gets his cat to do it."

"He does *sometimes* get citizens to do it, it's just . . ." Saori tailed off. "The *Mull of Kintyre*," she said suddenly.

Iona was surprised, but also elated, to hear these words.

"Clarence was the ship's cat," Saori went on, "and he didn't talk then. Why does he talk now?"

And in that moment Iona knew who their enemy was. Every human on the ship had been tested. Every one. But not every *living thing*. Iona wondered how she could even begin to explain it to Saori—there was too much to tell.

"Oh fuck," said Saori, looking from side to side in panic. "What have I done?"

They were interrupted by a loud *CRACK* coming from

the hallway and both of them turned to look. Saori stood, went to the door, and opened it—and she made no objection when Iona followed her.

They stepped into the corridor and found the guard at the door kneeling down next to the body of another citizen. The guard had twisted the citizen's arm off and was examining the joints like a doctor checking for broken bones.

Saori, who had never before seen the citizens' true nature, immediately turned and vomited against the wall. Iona approached the guard and asked: "What are you doing?"

The guard looked up at her. "Making a key."

———

Victor's cell was farther down the corridor and he was aware there was activity outside but he was too far away to hear what exactly was going on. His curiosity about this was such that when the door of his own cell opened he was pleased he'd get the opportunity to ask someone what was happening, and had momentarily forgotten that someone might be taking him away to be executed.

Saori walked in accompanied by a citizen, closed the door behind herself, and slid the grille shut so they couldn't be overheard. Victor started to ask Saori what the noise was but she held up a finger to her lips, walked over to him, and bent down to speak close to his ear.

"I'm told you understand how these work," she said.

And then she reached out and opened the hatch in the citizen's back.

11

VICTOR WAS PESSIMISTIC about their chances of success but Iona had more confidence. While it was challenging to program a citizen to enter a program into other citizens, Iona argued surely it was simpler if the program was intended to self-replicate? They'd talked about how to make it as straightforward as possible and minimize the possibility of error. They might only get one chance to do this. Victor didn't like the fact it involved replicating a mistake he'd made—it was always tricky to re-create circumstances you hadn't intentionally brought about—but he admitted it was their best chance.

Saori had told the rest of the bureau she needed to subject Victor and Iona to further interrogation and that she was not to be disturbed. Victor spent this time generating the program. Members of their citizen army were still in the other cells and Saori brought them to him as test subjects.

In the meantime Saori looked through her records regarding the population of the city and the business that went on there. Now that she knew most of the people

191

who lived here were wooden automata, she suspected she might be able to see clues as to who was human. She eventually found it in the plans of the city's sanitation system.

"Only the humans eat," Saori said as she brought the plans to Iona and Victor. "The citizens have batteries that are charged by a clockwork mechanism at the power plants. So only the humans have toilets in their homes and workplaces."

It was hilariously mundane. But clearly true. Victor asked how many other humans there were, based on this finding.

"Just one," Saori said.

They all knew who it was.

By now Victor's program was ready. He wanted more time to test it but Iona argued they couldn't afford to delay. The guard from her cell had made the key and it seemed likely that other citizens had made the same breakthrough or were close to it. When this happened Iona felt sure they would bring the key to Clarence.

Once the guard finished making the key, Saori and Iona took it off him and then disabled him by opening his hatch. Iona had watched the guard at work. It was grimly fascinating. He'd made the key with the nearest tools to hand—the component parts of one of his fellows. Having torn off the arm he had then cut it at the elbow, removed the citizen's head, extracted parts of its brain, and attached them to the arm. The resultant severed forearm, with electronic components spliced into it, was the key. Iona believed she understood how it worked. She hoped so.

Victor's program was entered into a fresh citizen, who was then released into the city. Citizen Zero. Saori left for King's Tower, and Iona and Victor waited in their cell while Citizen Zero did its work.

The king's lunch arrived, borne by one of his personal attendants. It struck him now that he should perhaps get someone else to taste it in case of poison but of course he couldn't ask them to do that, it was a disgusting idea. He could never suggest sharing food. It would be like suggesting they both sit in the same room and go to the toilet.

When Saori barged into the king's chambers while he was still eating, despite the attempted intervention of a guard, the king was furious and embarrassed. He spat the mouthful he was chewing into a corner of the room, then stood up and strode over to her.

"What do *you* want?" screamed the king. "Can't you see I'm—" And he stopped, reluctant even to admit to having been eating.

"I have to speak to you," Saori said.

"It can wait. This is outrageous."

"Shut up! We don't have long and this is more important than me walking in on you eating your fucking lunch."

The king didn't know how to react at all. Nobody spoke to him this way, not even—

"Where's Clarence?" said Saori at the very moment the king was thinking about his cat.

"Eating, I guess?"

"He's manipulating you—he gets you to run this whole city for his benefit, you understand?"

The king wanted to deny this. It felt like an insult, an accusation of weakness, that he'd let this happen all these years. But he didn't.

"But why though?"

"Because your cat is evil, Steve."

This is a hard thing for anyone to accept. Despite what Alyssa had said to him, despite his mounting suspicions in recent days, the king didn't want to believe what, deep down, he knew.

"It isn't even your cat," said Saori. "It's a thing that takes over bodies and kills the mind of what's inside. It killed your cat and took his place back when we were still on the ship."

This had the desired effect. "Yeah," said the king, nodding. "I think it did kill my cat. I . . . don't think I want to be king anymore. Bloody hell—you *were* on the ship too, weren't you—"

"Steve, there's no time—we have to leave. Clarence is trying to get out—"

"Get out of the tower?"

"No no—out of the *city*."

"Out of the . . ." For a moment he didn't understand, then he remembered there was something beyond the woods, something beyond the sky: so much more. He remembered steering ships through deep space, the infinite vacuum. He remembered it had once been his favorite thing. It had been his *life* and he'd forgotten it completely, agreeing instead to spend his life signing off paperwork in a room at the top of a tower. All this time he'd felt frustrated somewhere at the back of his mind, and it was because living here was like being in the cockpit of a rocket that never took off. As they built more floors on top of it he got higher and higher but never actually left the ground. And meanwhile he kept on building this city as if it was their destination and he'd get there eventually.

"Can *we* get out?" he said to Saori.

"I don't know, but we're going to try—but we *can't* let Clarence out."

"Okay," said the king, taking off his crown and tossing it out of the nearest window. Then he followed Saori and left his chambers for the last time.

————————

Iona and Victor had given it about twenty minutes before leaving the cell at the bureau. Iona held the key. They were unsure what they'd find outside the cell, whether Citizen Zero had been effective. But as they descended it was clear the bureau was empty. Everyone had left the building.

"It's worked," said Iona.

"So far," said Victor.

They walked out through the unguarded front door and into the streets. The mood was already distinctly different. It was easy to tell at a glance which of the citizens had fallen victim to the new program and which had not. The reprogrammed ones were alert, focused, purposeful—and devoid of individual character. They all had only one thought now: to find others of their own kind and change them as they'd been changed. A reprogrammed citizen would stop another citizen, open the hatch in its back, and replicate the program. Then they would both go in search of another, so the rate of change was speeding up exponentially. Iona felt thrilled and a little scared to realize it was unstoppable now.

Iona told herself the citizens weren't people, that their personalities had been programmed in the first place—but those personalities had been shaped further by countless days of experience, just like any human being, and they were being rapidly washed away. There was nothing else to be done—it was impossible to get all the citizens out and even if just one was left behind it might hold the plans for the key and supply the Poramutantur with one. But as Iona watched it happen she realized she'd always regret it.

Assuming she survived, of course.

Nobody paid Iona or Victor any mind as they made their way to the tower, where they'd agreed to meet Saori at the entrance. There was no sign of her. If she'd been successful in getting the king out then she should be there by now. Saori had told them that in this eventuality they should move on to the second phase without her. But now as they were facing this prospect Iona didn't like it at all.

"She might need help," said Iona. "Someone should go in."

Victor glanced through the open doors of the tower. "Alright. Who?" It was plain he didn't want to and didn't want to admit it. He'd been much more confident at the bureau with his army of citizens around him. Now it was just the two of them.

"I'll be as fast as I can," said Iona, handing the key to

Victor and stepping inside the tower.

The program was spreading through the building. The citizens were all focused on each other and didn't even register Iona as she walked through the lobby. The huge spiral stairwell at the center, which was usually well guarded, was completely open. It seemed too good to be true.

But after a moment's thought she realized it didn't matter if it was too good to be true. She had to go up the stairs regardless. At this point every option might easily end in her death. She told herself this was a liberating state of affairs, in a way, as she started to climb.

———

Iona realized something was wrong as she approached the eleventh floor. Until now every floor she had passed had been occupied by citizens reprogramming each other and then looking for more citizens. Sometimes they passed Iona on the stairs as they ran out of citizens to convert on one floor and went up or down looking for more. Iona had called Saori's name at each floor: she wondered if she ought to call the king's name as well but she worried shouting "Your Highness" might attract the wrong sort of attention.

Confirmation that something was wrong arrived when

the severed head of a citizen rolled down the stairs past her and she had to dodge otherwise it would've hit her on the shin. The head was followed by the body, which almost knocked her off her feet.

Iona looked up. She could hear scuffles coming from a higher floor. The sound of wood connecting with wood. And then another citizen—this one with its head still attached to its shoulders, but with a splintered left leg—came tumbling down toward her. It was trying to stand but was too badly damaged. Iona gripped the handrail and pulled herself close to the wall but as the citizen continued its uncontrolled descent its head collided with hers. A dazed Iona clung to the railing, unable to focus: for a moment she could only tell which way was up and which was down from the sound of the citizen still falling away from her while the conflict continued somewhere above.

As Iona prepared to go on climbing, a citizen ascended the stairs past her with the blandly determined countenance of the reprogrammed. She tried to warn it of the danger ahead but it wasn't listening because they had programmed it not to listen. Iona walked up behind it—if she couldn't divert it from its path then she could at least use it as a shield. Which seemed brutal but there it was.

Just before the door to the twelfth floor, Iona and her

shield encountered a row of citizens lined up on the same step, with another row behind them and more rows behind that, going back farther than Iona could see—the twist of the staircase took them out of view. The steps immediately below the citizens were littered with the bodies of more citizens, and those in the front rank kicked the bodies away down the stairs.

The citizen who was walking up ahead of Iona approached the massed ranks, and as per its programming, tried to engage the nearest one so it could reprogram it. The reaction to this was a flurry of wooden fists. The reprogrammed citizen managed to stand its ground for a moment but one of the citizens opposing it grabbed its shoulders, dashed its head against the wall, and let it fall back onto the steps.

Iona stepped aside and let it roll past. Then she looked up at the ranks of citizens. They looked back at her. They didn't address her, they didn't come to her, they just waited for her to approach.

"Could you let me through, please?" said Iona.

"No," said the citizen who stood front and center.

"What's happening here?"

"There's a threat."

"Well *I'm* not a threat."

"She is," said a new voice from somewhere in the midst of the crowd. The citizens stood at attention as a large ginger cat slalomed between their legs and came to sit at the front.

This, Iona realized, must be Clarence. Now that she saw him, he did look familiar: the ship's pilot had owned a cat like this.

Another citizen made its way to the front of the crowd and stood behind Clarence. It held the severed forearm of a citizen with various robotic brain components plugged into it. Iona realized it would be wise not to let on that she knew what it was.

"She's a criminal," Clarence continued, addressing his loyal citizens. "She plotted against the king and she was involved in the fire—"

"I know what you are," said Iona, knowing it might be dangerous to let him know this but she wanted to see his reaction. She added: "And I know what you're trying to do here."

"She is to be taken alive," Clarence continued, ignoring her. "I have an appropriate sentence in mind for her and her associates."

"What, burn us alive like you did Alyssa?"

"No, imprisonment. We'll have to design and build a prison, of course . . . I'd offer *you* the job, but . . ."

"You need us, don't you? Otherwise you'd have gotten rid of us years ago—"

"I don't *need* you."

"Then we're useful to you. You take over other people's bodies—if anything happened to that one, you might need a spare." Iona's thinking on this was evolving as she spoke. "But if you *could* switch to one of our bodies you'd have done it by now. It's the cage, isn't it? It keeps us all alive, stops us from aging—but it *also* means you can't leave that body. You're stuck as a cat. So you're keeping us alive for when you get out."

Cats can't shrug but Clarence created the impression of shrugging nonetheless. "You've worked it out again, then. I wondered how long it would take."

"What do you mean, again?"

"You've done this all before. The city was a great deal smaller then. But it was so long ago you've forgotten."

Iona wasn't sure if Clarence was making this up. Was he just trying to make her think she couldn't possibly beat him? That he would ultimately win no matter what she did?

"You could just agree to help me voluntarily," he went on. "That would be easier for all of us. I am trying to get us *all* out of here, you know."

"Help *you*? You killed my colleagues back on the ship—you *nearly* killed my wife and then almost drove her mad with suspicion and fear. You're not getting out of here. I can promise you, we're not—"

"Have a care, Ms. Taylor—I reiterate that I don't *need*—"

Then there was a commotion behind Clarence, farther up the stairs. Someone was pushing past the ranks of citizens, moving through them before they had a chance to react. Clarence turned just in time to see the king striding in his direction. Iona had never seen the king at such close quarters before: as Saori had said, he was human like the rest of them. And yes, she did recognize him as the pilot of their ship, the one who had owned the cat.

"You little *bastard*," said the king, bearing down on Clarence.

Clarence shrank back. "Your Highness, I'm dealing with a *mass* insurrection—it isn't safe, you must return to your—"

But the king ignored him, reached down, and grabbed Clarence by the scruff of the neck.

"Careful," Saori warned, pushing her way down the steps behind the king. "He's a murderer, remember."

Clarence hissed and spat, swinging his claws at the king, who held him at arm's length and flinched at each vicious swipe.

"He can't *do* anything," said the king. "He's just a cat."

"Get him *off* me!" said Clarence, appealing to the ranked citizens, who were still dumbly awaiting an order.

"No!" said the king, turning to those same citizens. "I order you *not* to do that."

But the citizens obeyed Clarence. They started to move.

"This way!" Iona shouted, pointing downward.

Saori and the king hurried down the steps toward Iona and together the three of them ran. The king still held Clarence by the neck and the cat still struggled to free himself. The king grabbed his legs and tried to hold him. The citizens had a steadier step and were gaining—but Iona heard footsteps coming up toward them—

More reprogrammed citizens were climbing the tower. Iona weaved between them and the king and Saori followed. The reprogrammed citizens were outnumbered by those loyal to Clarence but crucially their intervention slowed the loyalists down.

"I can't hold onto him much longer," the king said as he tried to keep the furious Clarence away from his head. The cat had made several deep cuts across his face. "I'm going to find a window and throw him out."

Clarence yowled and hissed.

"No!" shouted Iona. The reprogrammed citizens were still passing them on the steps. She weaved around them as best she could but she was slower than Saori or the king. "The fall won't kill him—we need to trap him somewhere while *we* get out—"

Iona stumbled on a dismembered citizen body, falling awkwardly. She may have been preserved by the cage but she was still a good deal older than the others. She was slowing them down.

Saori stopped to help her stand. The king turned and looked up the stairs, Clarence still struggling in his hands. He saw the citizens bearing down on them. The ranks were moving swiftly and they would inevitably catch up.

But then the king's face broke into a grin. "Wait—*yes*," he said. "This way!"

The king ran through the door that led to the eighth floor. Iona and Saori had no time to ask or even consider why. They followed him.

———————

Once Iona and Saori were through, the king slammed the door behind them, put the bolt in place, and then turned and looked around.

"Aren't we stuck in here now?" said Saori.

"No," said the king and walked on through the room. This had once been the kitchens. They'd been used for preparing his meals when the tower had been half its present size, but it was now twenty-three floors away from his quarters and by the time his food got there it would be lukewarm, so these kitchens had been abandoned and new ones installed farther up. The old kitchens had never been repurposed.

In the corner near the exterior wall was a stone oven.

The king opened the oven door. Clarence realized what was happening: he hissed and spat and threw himself around wildly.

"Help me!" said the king.

Iona and Saori joined the king at the oven. Iona held the door open while Saori helped subdue Clarence. The cat tried to bite and scratch them but they managed to push him into the opening and the moment the oven was clear of human hands Iona slammed it closed. There was no latch on the door so she kept her hands pressed against it while the king and Saori pulled a large, heavy table across the floor and lay it down so the top held the oven closed.

"Now what?" said Saori, panting. The citizens were battering on the door of the old kitchen and the bolt wasn't that strong.

The king pointed to the window. "That way."

Iona looked across and realized, of course—this entire side of the tower was covered in scaffolding. She wasn't sure if she was up to making the descent but the noises coming from behind the door and inside the oven compelled her to try. Without hesitating she followed the king to the window as he moved a chair over to it and climbed out. Iona stepped out after him.

Iona wasn't scared of heights and visited building sites all the time, but she'd never had to traverse one under this kind of pressure. She hurtled down ladders and across gangways, looking for handholds and keeping away from the open sides.

On the third floor, Saori, following close behind Iona, landed heavily on a weak plank and her foot went through it—she was stuck. Iona shouted for the king to wait. It was only then that she realized she didn't know his name.

The king saw Saori struggling and immediately doubled back to help.

"What was your name before you were the king?" Iona asked him while they pulled Saori's foot free of the broken boards.

"Steve," he said.

Of *course* it was.

By the time they reached the bottom Iona felt giddy from running back and forth across the scaffolding, and when she tried to race around to the entrance she was barely able to go in a straight line.

At the entrance they found Victor still waiting on the step, holding the key. He was jittery, he could hear something was going on in the tower and his relief at seeing them was evident. He started to ask how they'd gotten outside without first coming through the front door before realizing they didn't have time and it didn't matter: all that mattered was they were here. He asked if they were ready.

"Yes," said Iona.

Victor attracted the attention of the nearest citizen, milling around looking for someone to reprogram, and said to it in a clear voice: "You are dead."

When the citizen heard this specific trigger phrase it started to walk through the city, repeating it loudly. While it did this it placed its wooden palms together and rubbed them against each other rapidly and tirelessly. It took a minute or two for this action to start a fire. Once the fire caught, the citizen headed into the nearest building so that would catch fire too.

The trigger phrase passed from citizen to citizen, across the city, and they all reacted the same way. The fires spread quickly and because everybody was occupied with starting the fires there was nobody to put them out. Iona worried the plan might be *too* effective, leaving them insufficient time to escape. It was by no means clear the key would work anyway, it hadn't been tested. But the important thing was to destroy the city and its citizens so the Poramutantur couldn't get out.

If they died, well . . . they had all lived too long anyway.

Iona, Victor, Saori, and Steve ran through the burning streets together—the first time the four of them had been together in as long as they could remember. Something about it felt right to Iona—they belonged together.

Of course there had been many more crew members on board the *Mull of Kintyre,* so they might only have been on nodding terms during the mission itself. But after the crash they must have been thrown together, fighting for survival. They felt like a unit, and they were finally working as one.

The heat from all the fires was building up and they had to keep running but Iona was tiring. She took a moment to rest and glanced back over her shoulder at the tower. People had always assumed King's Tower was her proudest achievement but that wasn't true: she preferred buildings with function and the tower actually *did* very little. The fire was surging up it at a considerable rate.

Steve saw her looking and he stopped and turned to look too. It had been his home since he'd been made king—a position he'd only been given because the ship's cat belonged to him and this made him the easiest person to manipulate.

As they watched, the base of the tower weakened to the point where the structure could no longer support itself. Once it started to lean it all happened very quickly—people talk of large buildings collapsing as if in slow motion but that's not what this was like. It fell away from them and was gone almost in the blink of an eye.

Iona and Steve looked at each other. He looked bewildered, panicky: he hadn't yet come to terms with what had happened. But Iona felt nothing. If anything she felt relief.

Victor and Saori were shouting at them to keep running so Iona and Steve turned and carried on. Smoke was washing across the streets and they had to trust they'd set off in the right direction because they couldn't see where they were going. Iona only realized they'd reached the edge of the city when she felt the grass under her feet. Eventually the smoke cleared and they were climbing a gentle ridge toward the woods, at the top of which they allowed themselves to stop, turn, and look.

There was nothing to see except fire and smoke. In the blaze the city had lost its shape. The place they'd lived all this time—the only place any of them could clearly remember—was gone and none of them knew if they could get to anywhere else.

Exhausted now, they dragged themselves on through the woods and found their way to the window. The attention of the figures had been attracted by the fire. None of them were doing anything about it: it was hard to tell if they were even concerned, or if they were just observing. Perhaps they assumed this was normal, that the life cycle of the human was to build a vast city and eventually burn it down.

When the humans got out—if they got out—they'd have to deal with the figures' reaction, whatever it might be. The figures might simply shoot them. From their point of view they were just animals escaping their cage.

Iona was at the back of the group when they arrived at the window but she made her way to the front and Victor handed her the key. They'd agreed she would be the one to open the door, or at least try to. The door wasn't visible but Iona knew where it was—about a meter to the left of the window. She stepped over to the blank wall, raised the key—

And a dark, perfectly straight vertical crack opened in the wall, about two meters tall. It grew wider until it was enough to walk through. Standing in the doorway was a figure.

Iona hadn't used the key yet.

The figure was pointing something at her, something that might be a weapon; Iona couldn't tell. It was black and looked like a twisted tree root.

The four humans froze. Iona felt sure it was about to kill them.

It didn't kill them. It took a step back, making space for them to come through. Behind them the city was burning, the smoke was seeping out through the doorway.

Iona walked out of the cage.

12

THE FIGURE KEPT WALKING backward, its attention fixed on the humans, pointing the twisted black thing at them.

"Is it a weapon?" said Saori to her colleagues in a low voice that broke into coughing.

"Let's assume it is for now, shall we?" said Iona. All four of them had just been running as fast as they could through a smoke-filled environment. They all needed medical attention but the chances of communicating this to the figures seemed slim.

In the meantime the door of their cage was still open and smoke was seeping through it and there was always the chance of the Poramutantur getting out. Iona ushered the others forward and said to the figure, "You *must* close the—" before the door closed behind them.

Iona breathed out: their primary goal was achieved. Now to see if they could stay alive.

The room they were in was dark and lined with dimly lit instrument panels. Either the figures didn't need much light to operate or they'd kept the lighting levels low so the inhabitants of the cage wouldn't be able to see what they were doing in there.

The figure kept walking backward. None of the four humans made any sudden movements. None of them wanted to startle the figure. Iona was aware her attempts to read its body language might be completely wide of the mark—its social signifiers were probably very different from her own—but it seemed as though it didn't trust them. This reading of the situation seemed to be consistent with how it had kept them in a cage for hundreds of years.

Two other figures were in this room and they moved to walk behind the one who'd let them out. Like the first figure they walked backward. (Unless they were actually walking forward? She had to take care not to make assumptions.) The humans kept moving toward them, keeping the distance between them more or less the same.

"Are they leading us somewhere?" Saori murmured between coughs. She was sounding pretty bad and Iona was wondering about her own condition. The cage had been keeping them all alive. Things could be very different now that they were out.

"Should we stop walking and see what they do?" asked Victor.

Iona was about to agree when one of the figures operated a control and the door to the outside opened. The figures kept walking backward, out through the door. The humans followed.

———

Outside it was cold. Not *very* cold but colder than the humans were dressed for and cold enough to sting their smoke-irritated airways. The city had no seasons and its weather was consistently mild. Iona had only ever been aware of changeable weather as a dream concept: she had dreamed of storms, for example, and snow, but never experienced either. The sky above them was gray and cloudless and the sun hung low, shining weakly at them. It seemed to be morning here. In the city it had been afternoon.

They were walking along a pathway made of something that looked like concrete with a layer of rubber on top—materials that were familiar to Iona but which she had not seen for as long as she could remember. She felt surprised that she recognized them at all. The ground on either side of the pathway was stony and scrubby. The earth was a very dull, faded violet color.

The pathway split off and went in several different directions. Each fork of the pathway led to a large dome, maybe fifty or sixty meters high, with a smooth, dullish, off-green surface broken only by a small door. From where Iona stood she counted eight of these domes—quite possibly there were more out of sight—and she noted the thing she had just stepped out of was one of them. What Alyssa had said was true—the dome they'd been in *was* larger on the inside. Iona felt fascinated and wanted to know how it was done.

She wondered if she would get a chance to ask.

The three figures who had led them outside were still backing away. They addressed each other in noises that were presumably their language: a series of low, clicking sounds. When they reached the first fork on the pathway they stopped.

The humans took this as their cue to stop, at which point Iona fully appreciated how tired she was. She had a terrible headache and the adrenaline was no longer enough to prop her up.

"What now?" said Steve, who didn't sound healthy either. Victor tried to reply but broke into coughing before he managed to say anything intelligible.

There was movement at the edges of Iona's vision. The four humans turned to see six figures hurrying across the ground between the pathways. The humans tensed, assuming an ambush was imminent. But instead the six figures all poured into the humans' dome before closing the door behind themselves.

The humans turned back to look at the three figures on the pathway. The one holding the thing that was probably a weapon took a small step closer and said in a smooth, mannered voice: "We have nowhere to put you."

None of the humans had expected it to speak English, or anything they could recognize. It had spoken it oddly, putting emphasis in places no native speaker would, but it was English all the same. Iona was very surprised, but the fact she passed out a few seconds later had nothing to do with surprise. She passed out from exhaustion. The surprise was just a coincidence.

Her last thought as she slumped to the walkway was *They're going to put me in another bloody cage, aren't they?*

———

Iona woke in a pale yellow room with no windows. Slowly she became aware of figures moving around her and at first she thought she was dreaming because they seemed to be walking up and down the walls. Then she realized she didn't know anything about these beings and maybe they could walk on walls. Gradually she realized *she* was the one on the wall. She lay in a bed that had its own gravity, variable according to what suited the occupant, and it had been mounted vertically for reasons she didn't immediately understand.

Circular patches were stuck to her arm and abdomen. Tubes and wires trailed off from these patches, connecting her to sleek machinery mounted on the wall to her right. The clothes she'd been wearing upon leaving the dome had been removed at some point and replaced with loose-fitting black pajama-type garments. They weren't terribly comfortable.

The memory of what had happened came back to her. Her body tensed up as she realized she was still a captive of these creatures. She could tell it was not possible to get out of the bed. If she dangled a foot off the side the gravity automatically increased, preventing her from rising. They had indeed put her in another cage.

Iona breathed deeply and felt a pain in her chest but it wasn't the pain she was expecting. Her lungs didn't protest—they seemed fine—however there were needle-like sensations across her ribs, in the skin and the bones. She touched a hand to her chest and found a scar right down the center of it. The scar was very tender, though it felt very clean.

She wondered how long she'd been unconscious.

The figures around her noticed she was awake. Until this point they'd been acting like she wasn't there: now they began to act like they were far too aware of it. Two figures attended to the machines to her right. Another figure stood directly in front of the bed and addressed her. She couldn't tell if it was the same one that had led them out of the cage—she had yet to find any way of distinguishing the figures from each other—but it was holding the same device, the thing that might be a weapon, and was pointing it at her.

The bed's gravity field made Iona feel like she was looking up at the figure. It was a strange and unpleasant way to hold a conversation but she was determined not to let on that she felt discombobulated.

The figure seemed to be waiting for her to speak. From its point of view it must have been like talking to a portrait hanging in a gallery.

"How are the others?" Iona said.

"They are being restored," the figure replied.

"Does that mean they're alright?"

"They will be."

Iona pointed at her chest. "What happened here?"

"Damage. Extensive. We replaced the relevant parts."

Iona's eyebrows raised. "Replaced?"

The figure pointed at the wall opposite Iona and a diagram appeared on it—a cutaway of the human body with all organs visible. The lungs and other parts of the respiratory system were highlighted.

"You replaced all *that*?" said Iona.

"Yes."

"With . . . what?"

"Organic component replication. We took a sample of your DNA and used it to grow replacement parts."

Iona considered this: it wasn't an entirely strange idea. She felt like this technique had existed on Earth. Yet she still found it unsettling that pieces of herself had been substituted for identical pieces. She wondered where her old lungs were now but didn't like to ask.

"You know a lot about us, don't you?"

"Yes."

"I mean, you speak our language."

"We have been watching you for a long time." This was true. The figures had been looking at them for so long without ever trying to communicate. It had never occurred to Iona that they could have done so but chose not to.

"Have you put me in one of the other domes?"

"No."

Iona waited for an elaboration on this statement. None arrived. "Where are we then?"

"A medical facility. You burned the habitation deliberately. You put yourselves at great risk." The phrasing was neutral but Iona still felt like it was a criticism.

"We did burn it deliberately, yes—"

"To force us to open the door."

"What? No."

"You knew we could not let you die."

Iona found this information interesting. "We didn't know that, actually."

"But you burned the habitation." Iona noticed the figure didn't ask questions. Instead it made statements that implied a request for information.

"We burned it because there was something dangerous in it."

"*You* are dangerous."

"We're not dangerous."

"We know you are dangerous."

"Something more dangerous than us." A terribly urgent thought occurred to her. "You haven't let it out, have you?"

"You mean the fifth human?"

"No, not her—"

"Your fellow killed the fifth human after we placed it in there with you."

If they knew about this they had indeed been watching activity inside the dome closely. Iona wondered how they'd kept such close tabs on them—tiny drones perhaps?—but there were other things to worry about right now.

"No," she said, "there was a cat. You know, the small creature." Iona used her hands to vaguely suggest the size and shape of Clarence. She expected skepticism from the figure but it seemed to take this at face value.

"Nothing emerged from the habitat except you and the other three humans."

"You *can't* let it out. See, it *made* Steve kill Alyssa. That's what it does, it gets inside your head—if you let it out it'll do the same thing out here."

"Nothing more will emerge from the habitat."

"Good," said Iona, relieved.

"The habitat has been reset to default."

"And . . . what does that mean?"

"The matter comprising the habitat has been re-processed into energy."

"We did most of that job for you already," muttered Iona—then a thought occurred to her. "Wait—*all* the matter?"

"Yes."

"Including our spaceship?"

"The spaceship was nonfunctional."

"We still might've wanted it."

"All matter comprising the habitat has been re-processed."

Iona was surprised by how deeply she felt the loss of the *Mull of Kintyre.* She'd only remembered its existence very recently but it had come to stand for the life she'd lost. Burning the city she'd lived in as long as she could remember had been difficult to accept but she *had* accepted it. Losing the ship, broken and ruined as it was, felt harder to accept.

But the figures had done the right thing. They'd resolved the issue in the cleanest possible way. Just blitzed everything inside. It was all gone.

"Can I go outside, please?"

———

The figure advised Iona to keep to the walkways. It didn't say what would happen if she stepped off the sides and Iona didn't want to ask, although she noted it was still pointing that weapon at her.

The figure had informed her two days had passed since they'd stepped out of the dome. The days here were roughly three hours longer than days in the city, which had presumably been attuned to the humans' natural rhythms. It was afternoon, and quite sunny, but still a little cold.

The medical facility was located in a space between two of the domes. As she walked between them Iona noticed something she'd been too distracted to absorb the last time she was here: the domes were located in a shallow canyon, its sides only a little higher than the domes themselves. Steps had been carved at regular intervals along the sides, leading up out of the canyon.

Iona still felt anger at the figures for holding them all

captive but she had to keep it in check. Aggression would not help the situation. Understanding it might. She still had little idea of what was going on or why.

"These other ones," said Iona, pointing at the domes around them, "are there humans in them too?" She held out some hope that more of the *Mull of Kintyre*'s crew had survived the crash.

"No, they contain the other life of this planet," the figure said.

Iona stopped walking. "What other life?"

"Other life." The figure pointed the weapon upward and operated a control. In the air directly above the muzzle an image appeared of something dark brown and birdlike, with no beak and wings at least five times the length of its body. This image was replaced by one of a shaggy creature that looked like an antelope covered in grass cuttings. Then a long-limbed insect-looking thing with twelve legs, six of which were on its back. There were more.

Iona realized the thing wasn't a weapon at all. It was a device for displaying visual recordings, which meant . . . it probably also *made* visual recordings. That was why the figure had been pointing it at her all this time, it was keeping a record.

Something of the situation clicked into place for Iona.

"I think you've made a mistake," said Iona gently. "That's the native life of this planet." She didn't know this for certain but none of the creatures looked familiar; she didn't get that flash of recognition she usually did when encountering something from the old world.

The figure shut off the images (it had shown at least a dozen by this time) and pointed the recording device back in her direction. "Yes. Protocol for preparation of a new planet. The terrain and atmosphere are to be made suitable where necessary. Prior to this, examples of native organic life are to be preserved."

"Yes, yes—" Iona felt sure she was right about this now. "And that's why you said you couldn't let us die. I understand all that but we're *not part* of the native organic life."

"You were here when we arrived."

"But we came here for the same reason as you, to set up a colony. We were both looking for life-supporting planets in this area—if we had similar criteria of *course* we'd both choose the same one. You've colonized our colony!"

The figure didn't confirm or deny any of it. Iona wasn't sure if it was still processing what she'd said or just had nothing to say.

"You see," she continued, "you just swept us up with everything else. And the ship was in there—you probably built it around us, didn't you—" Iona stopped and looked around. "But if you can do all this, if you're so advanced . . . why didn't you realize we're not native to this planet? Wasn't the spaceship a clue?"

"The presence of the spaceship was noted and reported to the deciders."

Iona raised her eyebrows. "Deciders?"

"Yes."

"Who are the deciders?"

"They define the protocols. Everything is clear."

"They're like . . . your bosses?"

"Yes. Anomalies are reported to the deciders."

"So the buck stops with them. Okay. I'd like to see them."

"You cannot. None of them are here."

"Where are they then?"

"At home."

———

The figure led Iona up a set of steps that led out of the valley and onto a bleak, dusty plain. A large transparent sphere stood incongruously on the soil. Suspended in the center of the sphere was a loosely humanoid creature that somewhat resembled the figures, but its body seemed more refined, made up of intricate threads in shades of brown and gray. And unlike the figures it wore clothing—a loose-fitting dark green plastic-looking garment. Set into its head, about where a human's cheekbones would be, were two large black eyes. Iona couldn't tell if it had a nose or mouth: if it did they were probably concealed under the fronds that made up its skin. The figures looked like what you'd get if you left this being to melt slightly in the sun. Iona and the figure stopped in front of it and looked up.

"This was our assigned decider," the figure said.

Iona realized this was a memorial. The body had been preserved and left on display, as if watching over the figures. "What happened to . . . it?"

"It died from an illness during the journey. We reported back to homeworld expecting a replacement to be sent."

"But they didn't send one? They just left you to run the whole operation?"

"Their presence is only necessary for policy decisions. We are capable of performing all functions. Mineral deposits are delivered via the haulage chain."

Iona blinked. "You're stripping this planet."

"And we will return it, as far as possible, to its natural state when we are finished."

"I thought you were here to research it."

"Research is a subsidiary activity. The focus is mineral extraction."

"And you reported our presence to these deciders."

"Yes."

"And they told you to keep us locked up?"

"They did not respond. In the absence of guidance we treated you as native life. The protocols were clear."

"Have you reported to them that we're outside the dome now?"

"We report all unusual activity."

"Did you report Alyssa's arrival?"

"Yes."

"And did they reply?"

"No."

"Have they ever replied?"

"No."

"In all the centuries since you came here and set up this . . . operation, you've had no contact from them at all?"

"No. In the absence of further instructions, we continue until the planet is exhausted. The protocols are clear."

———

That evening Iona stood in the observation room of the dome that had previously housed the city and looked through the window into the off-white interior. So many times she'd stood on the other side of this window looking at figures, believing the world beyond the window was so much smaller than the world she lived in. But her world had always been tiny, and now it didn't exist at all.

The dome had been shut down but Iona could tell the figures were still considering whether to reactivate it and put the humans back in once they were fully recovered from their injuries. She was preparing her argument that the figures' protocols didn't say they had to do this because the humans were not native life, and if their protocols said they didn't have to do something then they shouldn't do it. Iona rehearsed this argument repeatedly: it dominated her thoughts. But she was aware that if one followed this to its logical conclusion, the only reason the figures were keeping the humans alive was the protocols told them to preserve the native life. The humans would be left to fend for themselves and Iona was not at all confident they could. The figures would be reluctant to share any of this planet's resources. Their protocols told them their primary function was to strip the place, and if the humans took even a small portion of what was here this could easily lead to conflict. Her ideal scenario—in which she convinced the figures to adapt one of the craft in their supply chain into a vehicle capable of making the trip to Earth—seemed remote indeed.

Iona walked outside and found Victor sitting on the ground, leaning against the outer wall of the dome. After her conversation with the figure up on the plain she'd spoken to the other humans and explained the situation. Their reactions had varied. Steve in particular had reacted with anger: like Iona he'd demanded to speak to the deciders, but when told he couldn't he raged at the figures for dumbly following orders. Saori had convinced him to calm down, rightly arguing their position with the figures was still precarious. But Victor had been quiet.

As Iona sat down next to him he started with surprise, and she realized he'd been lost in thought. She asked if he was alright.

"Yeah," he said. "I was just thinking about them guys." He jerked his thumb in no particular direction but it was clear he meant the figures. "Going on doing the job, following their little protocols, sending back the loot, keeping the supply chain going. But there's nobody out there, is there?"

"We don't *know* that," said Iona. "Maybe there is and they just don't care. Maybe they just can't be bothered to come out here and deal with it."

"Well exactly. It's not the people who sent them that I'm sad for. I'm sad for *them*. Poor bloody simple creatures."

"They seem engineered for the purpose."

"Oh obviously, yeah. Engineered not to be too curious and just carry out instructions. Just going on and on until someone tells them to stop."

"Maybe they're happy doing that."

"Nah," said Victor, gesturing at a figure as it crossed the space between the domes. "You see how interested they are in us? They've been watching everything we do all this time."

"Yes, because they were told to research the native life—"

"They've had us in there *centuries*, they know all they need to know by now. They kept watching us because they got something out of it. Something they don't get in their normal lives."

Iona hadn't thought of it like that. If Victor was right, that made it a great deal more likely that the figures would put them back in.

13

THE HUMANS CONTINUED TO live in the medical facility, sleeping in their vertical beds at night. But only
the figures' innate caution had stopped them from
dealing with the issue of what to do with them sooner,
or at least this was what Iona believed. She told her colleagues as much one day during a long conversation
after lunch. Iona was reluctant even to say all this out
loud, because she felt sure the figures were listening to
them and she didn't want to give them any ideas, but
she needed to work out how to tackle this before it all
came to a head.

"Look, we *are* smarter than them," said Saori. She
leaned back in her chair and rested her feet on the alu-
minum table they'd been given to use at mealtimes. Her
shoes made a dull ringing sound as they made contact
with the surface. After centuries of only using wooden
furniture they all found the noise jarring—except Saori,
who seemed to revel in such noises and made them quite
deliberately. "I refuse to accept we can't argue our way
past them."

"We need them to give us a ship," Iona said. "That's the bottom line."

"We need more than just a ship," said Steve. "We can't use the wormhole, obviously, and I worked out the journey time. The kind of propulsion their ships use, you're looking at eighty-seven years."

"Okay, so we also need a suspension system to get us there alive. Considering the technology we've already seen, they must have something like that."

"But they won't give *us* any of it," said Victor. "They're wedded to their protocols and giving us a ship acts against the interests of their operation."

"It's so stupid," said Steve. "It's so obvious these deciders are all dead. This disease that killed off their boss probably carried off the others too."

"That's all supposition—" Iona began.

"But for the purposes of argument," Saori interrupted, "it is *overwhelmingly* likely they're all dead. Those guys have sent multiple reports saying things aren't right here—and in return, no visit, not even any guidance on how to deal with it. And these deciders seem like they *love* giving out instructions, so yeah, I'm going with 'they're all fucking dead.'"

Iona wondered if Saori had always been this abrasive or if life in the city had made her this way.

"But if they *are* all dead," Iona said, "what difference

does that make to us?"

"If we can make the figures *see* what they're doing here is pointless—"

"So you want to undermine the entire underpinnings of their existence."

"Well, their existence is—"

"I think that's an incredibly risky thing to do."

"It might be the kindest thing to do," said Victor. "They're working their arses off, tearing this planet to pieces for nothing. Everything they've mined is probably just piling up back on their homeworld."

"But we've no idea how they might react," said Iona. "It could be like proving to someone their god doesn't exist. They might treat it like blasphemy and put us to death."

"Or they might go totally nihilistic, and I dunno, kill us and go on a rampage across the galaxy," said Steve.

"Exactly," said Iona, grateful for the support. "I don't think it helps us at all."

"Confronting someone with the truth," said Saori, "is never the wrong thing to do."

"That just isn't true."

"So you'd rather Alyssa hadn't told you the truth, back in the city?" asked Victor.

This argument was still going on (and Iona was worried she was losing it) when a group of figures urgently entered the facility. Iona's first thought was this was it, the figures had made their decision and were putting them back in their cage. But it quickly became clear the humans were not the focus of this activity. In fact it seemed as if the humans had been forgotten entirely.

———————

The figures had gathered in one of the rooms of the medical facility: rather a lot of them, in fact. The room was heaving as the figures jostled for a view of what was happening at the other side of it, where the bed was. They chattered urgently and some at the front seemed to be admonishing the others, demanding to be given space. Iona had never seen them act like this: they were neither calm nor cautious.

All four of the humans managed to squeeze in at the back of the room but none of them could see much. Iona found a storage crate in the corner that looked like it would take her weight, stepped on it, and peered over the figures' heads.

The creature in the bed looked a lot like the decider up in the glass sphere on the plain. Its clothes were different but it was evidently the same species. Iona was about to relate this information to the others when the decider's eyes opened.

Every figure in the room kneeled and inclined their

heads toward the new arrival. This supplicant pose rippled through the crowd, leaving just Iona, Saori, Victor, and Steve standing.

The decider stared back at the humans blankly.

Iona stepped down off the crate.

———————

When the figures had finished bowing down to the decider they noticed the humans were there. One of the figures—Iona thought it was the one who'd released them from their cage—suggested they return to the medical facility's communal area. It suggested this quite matter-of-factly, without a hint of threat, but when the humans asked it where the decider had come from and what was going on, it did not answer the questions. This was the first time it had ever declined to answer their questions. Instead it repeated its suggestion.

Saori, Victor, and Steve returned to the communal area. Iona said she was going to use the toilet, but instead she slipped out of the medical facility, walked up the steps out of the canyon and onto the plain. She just wanted to check something.

At the top of the steps she saw the transparent sphere. The dead decider was still inside, its position unchanged from the last time she'd been here. It hadn't returned to life. So the one at the facility was new.

Iona walked up to the sphere and rapped her knuckle against it. Instead of a satisfying *ring* it made an odd, dull *glob.* It wasn't glass or anything like it. She wasn't sure what it was made of.

She walked back down the steps to the facility.

———————

The humans discussed the newcomer in low voices, ensuring the figures in the other room couldn't hear, even though the figures didn't seem to be paying them any attention.

"Bloody hell, they're *alive*," said Steve.

"Well," said Victor, "*one* of them is."

"This changes everything," said Iona.

"Yes, for the worse," grumbled Saori.

"I disagree."

"Oh, sorry, I hadn't realized that the arrival of the people who're responsible for locking us up was a cause for celebration."

"Don't go all sour grapes just because you were convinced they were extinct."

"That's not it at all—with the figures we were dealing with people less intelligent than ourselves who worked on strictly rational terms. Given time we'd have found a loophole in their protocols and convinced them—"

"I'm not sure we had time and I'm not sure there *is* a loophole."

"There's *always* a loophole. But now we're dealing with an acquisitive species, we've thrown a wrench in their plans and if they react emotively then—"

"I agree, we have to play this carefully but we *do* have a chance we didn't have before."

"Who put you in charge?" Saori said, then glared at Victor and Steve as if they might admit they had.

"I don't see you putting forward any solutions," said Iona, "you're just complaining everything's more difficult now."

"What I'm saying is"—and here Saori lowered her voice even more—"the decider is going to make a decision about *us*. And if it's not good . . . we might have to take action."

Steve nodded. "So do we wait for it to make the decision, or—"

"Attack it first?" said Iona.

"It's weak at the moment," said Saori. The decider was receiving medical attention, though the humans didn't yet know why.

"But the figures aren't and you saw how they reacted to it—they'd tear us to bloody pieces."

"We might not get a choice—"

"Wait wait wait," said Victor. "Alyssa told me this is what the Poramutantur did on all those other colonies. Got in people's heads and made them see threats and told them *get them first before they get you.* If we escape from it and then do the same thing, what was the point of it all?"

Nobody said much for a while. Saori glared at Victor occasionally and Iona thought she was going to take him to task for drawing the comparison. But she didn't.

When the decider finally came to see them it was a relief, even if Iona hadn't been looking forward to it.

It came to the doorway of the communal area, flanked by three figures. Iona couldn't be sure but she thought it likely they were the three who had been monitoring their dome when they'd been released. Certainly one of them held the same recording/display device and pointed it at the humans.

In the moments before the decider's arrival, Saori and Steve had been pacing the room anxiously; Iona and Victor had been sitting at the table. Victor stood reflexively, defensively perhaps. Iona stayed where she was.

The decider looked back at Iona. Was it expecting her to stand? Iona stuck to her guns—before the decider came in she had concluded that a nonconfrontational attitude would be the best approach and sitting down struck her as nonconfrontational. Unless it was expecting her to stand. In that case it might well seem confrontational. But she couldn't help how the decider interpreted her actions.

After a while the decider spoke, using the same language they had heard the figures use. But it didn't speak to the figures. It addressed the humans, who couldn't understand what it was saying.

Once the decider had finished speaking the figure with the recording device addressed them in English: "Have you been treated well?"

This was unexpected. It was the first time any of the figures had asked them a question, for instance. That alone told them the words had not originated with the figure: these were the decider's words, translated.

Iona was about to answer but, for the sake of harmony, decided to consult with her colleagues first. She turned to them.

They looked back at her. Saori shrugged.

Iona turned back to the decider. "Do you mean the whole time we've spent on the planet, or just the time since we got out of the dome?"

This question was relayed to the decider in its own language: it replied via the figure. "Both."

"Well," said Iona, "since we got out of the dome your people there saved our lives, fed us, and gave us somewhere to live, so no complaints there. Inside the dome . . ." She weighed this. She didn't want to be aggressive but she wanted to make clear what had happened to them and ideally imply a sense of obligation to do something about it. "We weren't harmed . . . but we *have* been kept there against our will for several centuries."

The decider listened and thought for a while. Eventually it made a statement that the figure translated.

"I am deeply sorry for the incarceration you have suffered at the hands of our drones. Please do not blame them. They were following the protocols set down for this operation."

Iona had expected to work a lot harder for this apology. She'd expected to have to make it understand that they were intelligent creatures worthy of consideration. Saori was nodding dumbly, looking a little stunned. Steve was blinking, close to tears. Sometimes you bore an ordeal without flinching and then crumpled at a minor act of kindness or even just an acknowledgment of what you'd been through.

"Where've you been all this time?" said Victor.

This was relayed to the decider, who replied via the figure: "I have only just arrived. My ship crashed. The drones found me in the wreckage and brought me here."

"But *why* have you only just arrived?" Victor continued in a terse, though level voice. Having just cautioned them all against antagonism he seemed to be struggling to keep his anger in check. "They sent reports. Loads of reports. They say you never replied until now."

"We have experienced difficulties."

Victor laughed when he heard this. The figures flinched. (The decider, Iona noted, did not flinch.) Victor covered his mouth with his hand, a little hysterical, but he collected himself. "Difficulties?" he said, nodding. "Is that right?"

"We have been at war," the decider replied. "Our enemies bombarded us with misinformation. We no longer knew what to trust. Anomalous messages and calls for assistance have been the basis of a large number of traps."

"But your supply line kept coming. I mean, your guys here say they send off their trucks and they come back empty."

"The supply line was intercepted. We believed this outpost was no longer operating."

"How long has this war been going on?" said Iona.

The decider conferred with the figure before answering: "Six hundred and twelve years."

"To be fair," said Steve, "that does sound like difficulties."

"So has this just ended now?" said Saori.

"No," the decider said, "the war has been over for some time. But reconnecting with all our outposts has been a long and difficult task. Our resources are much depleted by the war. This particular outpost was not considered a priority until—"

"Until you got the message about Alyssa turning up," said Iona.

"When we understood what was happening I was dispatched to investigate and revise protocols accordingly."

When none of the humans reacted to this the decider spoke again.

"I repeat my apology: I am sorry for your incarceration and take full responsibility on behalf of my ancestors who failed in their definition of the protocols. I have revised the protocols. The drones will give you every assistance to return to your own planet. They will convert one of the haulage chain vehicles into a ship capable of making the journey."

Iona stared at the tabletop. The decider was giving her exactly what she wanted. She couldn't have asked for any more.

"Is there anything else I can do?" asked the decider.

There were many things Iona wanted the decider to do, but she didn't think it could do any of them.

The decider apologized, saying it had a lot of work to do, assessing the various mining and processing operations elsewhere on the planet. It left the humans to absorb the knowledge their lives had been derailed by a mistake, a miscommunication. The entire civilization they'd built was an accident. None of it meant anything.

14

THE NEXT DAY, AFTER the decider had departed on its tour of the colony, something new appeared on the plain near the spot where the old decider, the dead decider, looked down from its sphere. Iona went up there to look at it.

None of the figures queried her presence. There had been a marked change in the figures' attitude toward them following the decider's intervention. Before, they had tried to pretend the humans didn't exist, though without neglecting them to the point where they died. They weren't sure how the humans fit into their framework. But now the decider had established how the humans fit and so everything was different. A group of figures now attended to the humans' needs to an almost oppressive extent. All the humans really wanted was to get out of here. Which was what the new thing on the plain was for.

The thing was one of the trucks that made up the figures' haulage line. It was a plain, gray, boxy object, about twenty meters high and sixty meters long. Four large thrusters were mounted on the rear end. The other three sides of the object were featureless, and although Iona couldn't see the top she was willing to bet it wasn't much more interesting. One curious detail was that it had rails on the bottom like a sleigh.

It was designed to carry nothing but consignments of minerals. It was entirely automated: nothing living had ever traveled in it, or at least nothing larger than a stray insect. It was filthy and had clearly been in service for some considerable time. Iona understood that the figures had the wherewithal to manufacture new vessels when a truck failed to return or broke beyond repair, but at present they did not have the materials in hand and would have to mine them, which would take time. Converting an existing one was much faster, they assured her. Looking at the aged crate that sat on the plain, Iona wondered whether she might prefer to wait.

Iona pulled up a box to sit on and watched the figures work for a few hours. There was nothing else to do, after all. She watched as they opened the hatch in the roof, which was for filling and emptying the container, and lowered a figure inside. She watched as they cut a rectangular panel out of one side and fashioned a doorway from it. She watched as they thoroughly cleaned the interior, rewired the automated control systems, and installed controls that could be accessed from the inside.

One of the figures came over to Iona and asked if it could get her anything to eat or drink. Iona asked for some water and fruit. The figure brought her both and she ate them in the sun. She could have done with some sunglasses, actually, but she guessed this was beyond the figures' capability to supply.

After a while she started to feel cold and made her way back to the medical facility, where she discovered Saori and Victor weren't speaking to each other. She didn't inquire why. If it hadn't sorted itself out by tomorrow she'd address it. They had a long journey ahead of them on that crate and she had no intention of playing mother to a bunch of squabbling kids.

––––––––––

The next morning Iona returned to the plain to find significant progress had been made overnight. Steve came with her. She wasn't sure if this was due to interest in the ship or a desire to remove himself from the conflict zone.

The truck had been fully lined on the inside with rubber-like tiles that could emit light where needed. In each corner a cubicle had been fitted that offered something similar to cryogenic suspension: thoughtfully the figures had placed these cubicles as far away from each other as possible and constructed small rooms around them to give them each some personal space within the tiny confines of the craft. At the front, in the gap between two of these cubicles, a basic two-dimensional screen had been mounted above the control panel. There were four chairs arranged in two rows of two, so if they wished they could all sit and be involved in piloting the craft. But this would largely be unnecessary as the ship's primary driver would be the automated controls it had originally been fitted with.

In the middle of the craft was a mess area with toilets, a machine that recycled water, and another that force-grew a protein-rich foodstuff that looked like tofu but was (as far as Iona could make out) made from something like plankton. The use of this should also be largely unnecessary, as the suspension system would keep them all alive without needing to eat for most of the journey to Earth.

"Just as well," Iona said to Steve. "I couldn't bear eating that stuff for decades on end."

"Ugh, no," Steve replied. They had both eaten a good deal of the protein while they were here. "It's not the taste, is it—"

"No, it doesn't really have a taste. It's the *texture*."

"Yeah, sort of . . . oily." Steve stuck his tongue out.

"I didn't want to say anything earlier," Iona laughed, "because I was worried about offending them." She indicated the figures who continued with the conversion work, paying them no attention at all.

Steve also laughed. "Don't be daft. They don't care, they're not like us."

"They don't *seem* like us. That doesn't necessarily mean—"

"They're just looking for someone to give them orders. They'd do anything if that decider told them to."

Iona was only half-listening by this point. She was thinking about the journey and what she'd said about "decades on end." During her time in the city she had forgotten how old she was, both in linear terms and physically. The figures' medical assessment had informed her that, physically, she was sixty-four years old. She wasn't sure how long humans usually lived but she knew she was not young. While she was in the city she'd frequently thought of her impending retirement that never arrived, and had been perfectly happy in that situation, doing something she enjoyed with nothing much left to prove. She'd given no thought to her time being limited because it wasn't. Things were different now. It was good to be free, but thinking of the future gave her a cold, anxious dread she'd never felt in the cage.

Steve was still talking about the figures in the same dismissive terms when Iona turned to him and said, "How long's the journey again?"

"What?" said Steve.

"The journey back to Earth."

"Dunno—sixty years, something like that?"

"That's not what you said the other day."

"Oh," said Steve, rubbing his eyes, "yeah—"

"It was more than that."

"Yeah, I think I might have gotten it wrong. I need to work it out again."

Iona nodded. "It could be fairly crucial," she said with a small laugh. "Make sure you get it right."

They stayed out there for a couple more hours, talking over the events of the last few days. Iona guided the conversation with care and listened to Steve's answers with keen interest.

———

By the evening the craft was ready and one of the figures invited Steve to come aboard and learn how to fly it. Iona decided to join him: "I mean, god forbid anything should happen to you," she said, "but if it does—"

"If it does you'll probably be best off trusting the autopilot to get you home," Steve said as they walked over to the craft. "I'm not even sure how much use *I'll* be—I can't even remember flying a ship."

"Muscle memory might come back."

"Let's hope so."

For over an hour Iona sat behind Steve and a figure,

watching them go over the controls and everything that might go wrong. The controls were a mixture of slick touch panels and clunky tactile levers and switches—the more basic they were the less there was to malfunction.

Finally it was time for a test flight.

Steve turned to Iona. "I think you should disembark."

"Why?"

"Because this crate might easily blow up three seconds after we leave the ground." He turned and addressed the figure. "No disrespect to your workmanship, mate."

"I'm sure it won't blow up," said Iona when the figure failed to mount a defense of the craft it had helped to make.

"Even if it doesn't," said Steve, "I might crash it, or the atmospheric pressure system might fail . . . Look, this is the whole point of doing a test flight."

"I'll take the risk."

"Yeah, well, I won't." Steve folded his arms and sat back. "I'm not taking off until you get off the ship."

The figure looked at Steve, then at Iona. It seemed a little distressed, unable to navigate the conflicting desires of two humans it had been instructed to serve. "It seems . . . you must disembark?"

Iona sighed, stood up, and walked toward the door of the craft. "Yes, alright. I'm perfectly confident it won't blow up, though."

When the craft took off Iona didn't turn to look at it. She was walking across the plain, back to the valley, and she had other things on her mind. As she'd predicted the craft did not blow up. She'd watched the figures put the thing together for the past two days and they struck her as a diligent bunch. She needed to go back to the medical facility and prepare for their departure.

———

It was late when the craft returned from its test flight.

Steve and the figure who'd instructed him disembarked. They agreed some tests would be run on the craft overnight, just to make sure no flaws had developed during the flight, and then the humans would leave tomorrow morning when it was light. Steve thanked the figure for its help and then walked down the steps that led to the valley and the medical facility.

He sensed something was wrong as he approached. The sun was setting but the lights inside the facility weren't on. Perhaps the other humans were all elsewhere? Some kind of farewell party thrown by the figures? He couldn't quite picture them doing that, but then who knew how they might have interpreted the new protocols that had been laid down.

He quietly opened the door to the facility and lingered

on the threshold. The entranceway was dark and silent. He wished the figure had come down to the facility with him. He wanted someone else to go inside first. But there was no one else around, not anywhere.

"Steve?" came a voice from within—Iona's voice. "Is that you?"

"Is everything alright, Iona?" he said. He couldn't see her. It sounded like she was in the communal area.

"Is anyone with you?"

"No."

Sounds of movement from inside. Iona appeared in the entranceway, her expression grim, and marched toward Steve. Before he could speak she strode past him and grabbed his wrist. "We need to go."

"Where?" said Steve as Iona pulled him back the way he'd just come, toward the steps. He pulled his arm away: her grip was hurting him.

"In the ship. We've got to get out of here."

"Now?"

"Yep."

"What about the others?"

Iona turned and faced Steve, a haunted, panicked look in her eyes. "Dead. Both of them. It's got out."

"What's got—You mean the Poramutantur?"

Iona nodded. "I don't know how—"

"But . . ." Steve swallowed. "Who—"

"Saori." Iona kept walking, urgently. "I don't know when it happened—"

"Shit. She *has* been acting a bit—"

"Maybe it happened when we were escaping from the tower; she was the last one out through the window, wasn't she? Maybe it got free from that oven—"

"But how do you *know* it's her?"

"She killed Victor. I saw her out behind one of the domes, burying the body—"

"But are you sure that means she's the Poramutantur?"

"Why else would she kill him? After all that's happened—"

"Maybe she just flipped."

"In that case she's a murderer and I'm *still* not traveling across space with her."

"What did you do when you saw this?"

"She hadn't seen me so I came back to the facility to wait for you." By now they had reached the steps leading out of the valley. On the way up Iona asked how the test flight had gone, if there were any issues.

"No," said Steve.

"Good, because if there were we'd be done for."

They reached the plain, and after Iona had looked back down the canyon to see if anyone was following them, they entered the craft. The figure who'd accompanied Steve on the test flight was still inside, ensuring everything was prepared for the journey. Iona told it to get out and it did so without question.

"Close the door behind yourself," Iona added as she and Steve took their seats.

As soon as the figure was a safe distance away the craft took off.

———————

Once they'd left the atmosphere neither of them wanted to talk about what they'd done. They watched as the planet receded from view, the place they'd both spent the last few centuries. The place where they were supposed to have built a new life, and in fact *had* built a new life, but not the one they were supposed to build, and which was gone now anyway. They didn't even know what the planet was called.

They went to the mess area and ate a meal, discussing what they would tell everyone when they got back to Earth. If nothing else the people there would want to know what had happened to Alyssa.

"I don't think we need to tell them about your part in it," Iona said with a heavy sigh, stirring her bowl of protein.

"I'd be very grateful," Steve replied. "I mean, it's up to you—"

"You weren't really in control, Steve. And we want them to focus on the important thing, which is coming back here and destroying that creature."

"You want to come *back*?"

Iona shook her head. "Not *me*, no. I just want them to send someone to deal with it. Of course, if it's in human form the figures will obey it, and it'll use that to its advantage . . . it's not going to be easy."

Steve nodded. "At least it's not our problem anymore."

———————

The suspension system's default programming was to wake its inhabitants once a year. This was a sensible precaution both for health reasons and to enable them to check the craft was running as it should. Of course, if there was an emergency the systems would wake them sooner.

Steve's suspension system woke him after two days. He rushed from the bay and into the empty cockpit.

The monitor was alive with what looked like analog static. In the midst of the static a cone seemed to be pointing directly at the viewer. In fact this was an illusion: the center of the image seemed to be the nearest point, when in fact it was the farthest away. It was a side effect of traveling through the wormhole.

But they weren't supposed to be in the wormhole at

all. After their previous journey the humans had accepted they couldn't travel through the wormhole again. Accordingly the craft was not designed to be able to travel this way. This was what had generated the emergency.

Steve went to turn off the autopilot, only to find it was turned off already. The nature of the wormhole was that you didn't need to steer—it was like being on rails. But it also meant you couldn't turn around: once you started a journey you had to finish it. He investigated whether there was any way of minimizing the damage the wormhole was doing to the craft, enough for it to survive until the other end. But he could already feel a tremor rising from the floor.

That was when he started to panic.

"I tried to stop it from waking you up," said Iona's voice from behind him.

He turned to see her leaning against the frame of the door to her suspension bay. She looked very calm, and that told him everything he needed to know.

"I was just going to let you sleep through the whole thing," she went on, "it seemed easier."

He strode over to Iona, grasped her around the throat with one hand, and pinned her to the wall. "Get the ship out of this or—"

"Or what?" She still seemed calm. "You'll steal my body like you stole Steve's? It's not going to be much good to either of us in a few minutes."

He glared back at her. He started to tell her she'd gotten it wrong, but she seemed to anticipate it and spoke over him.

"You didn't know the journey time to Earth. Steve wouldn't make a mistake about that."

He laughed. "What, that's *all* you're basing this on?"

"Oh no, that was just the start. We talked for a long time after that. You made a *lot* of mistakes."

He took his hand away. "So what you said about Saori killing Victor—"

"—was a lie, yes. Saori's just been in a funny sort of mood, culture shock probably, she's still herself. I told one of the figures to tell Saori and Victor I'd gone missing and take them on a wild-goose chase looking for me. Just needed them out of the way—the figure will have told them the truth by now. Useful how the figures do anything humans tell them to without question—I've got you to thank for that, haven't I? I mean *you* were the decider, weren't you?"

Steve remained silent.

"I reckon when the interior of the dome got reset," Iona went on, "you were still in there, because you can survive *anything*, can't you, and you took over one of the figures. You took DNA from the dead decider and used the figures' medical tech to grow a new body. The crashed ship where they found you was actually Alyssa's, maybe? Then you pretended to set off for some other part of the colony. But actually you stayed, and you took Steve." Her voice became unsteady with those last few words. "Did you choose him just because he was the one who shut you in the oven? Getting your own back, were you?" She looked up at him, waiting for confirmation.

He rushed at her and punched her in the chest. As she dropped to the floor of the craft she knew that if she'd gotten the story wrong he'd have taken pleasure in telling her so. But she was right so he was going to take pleasure in killing her instead. The shaking of the craft was getting more and more violent, its metal frame buckling under the pressure: there was little time left anyway. This small dark box would never reach Earth, and no one would ever know why she had left in it without Saori or Victor. No one would know what she'd died for. But that didn't matter. Everything got forgotten eventually anyway.

Iona barely felt the blows as they rained down on her. She'd already let go of everything. After all those long and meandering years in the city she was finally doing something meaningful.

She was still alive when the craft finally broke up. Her last thought was that the creature hadn't managed to kill her like it had killed Hanna. She'd chosen her own way out.

Acknowledgments

Thanks to Alan Barnes—this book started life as a pitch for something else a long time ago, and without him the idea would never have taken shape. It's changed a lot over the years and I'm surprised it's happened at all, but I'm very glad it has. Thanks to Mark Clapham, Lance Parkin, and James Cooray Smith for support and feedback, and thanks to Paul Cornell for his enthusiasm and inspiration.

Special thanks to Adam Christopher and to my editor, Lee Harris, and the biggest thanks of all to Catherine Spooner, without whom none of this would be possible.

About the Author

© Sami Kelsh

EDDIE ROBSON is a novelist, scriptwriter, and journalist. His first novel, *Tomorrow Never Knows,* was published in 2015. His other credits include the BBC Radio sitcom *Welcome To Our Village, Please Invade Carefully; Adulting,* the Guardian's first original drama podcast; *The Space Programme,* the first radio soap opera for children; episodes of the Chinese adaptation of *Humans;* and animated shows including *The Amazing World of Gumball* and *Sarah & Duck.* He has also written numerous spin-offs from *Doctor Who* and comic strips for *2000 AD.* He lives in Lancaster with his wife and two children.

TOR·COM

**Science fiction. Fantasy. The universe.
And related subjects.**

*

More than just a publisher's website, *Tor.com*
is a venue for **original fiction, comics,** and
discussion of the entire field of SF and fantasy,
in all media and from all sources. Visit our site
today — and join the conversation yourself.